ULYSSES
~Comin' Home~

THE STORY OF A DOG'S IMPOSSIBLE ODYSSEY
TO BE REUNITED WITH THE FAMILY HE LOVES

Simon Christopher Dew

 FriesenPress

Suite 300 - 990 Fort St
Victoria, BC, V8V 3K2
Canada

www.friesenpress.com

Copyright © 2021 by Simon Christopher Dew
First Edition — 2021

All rights reserved.

No part of this publication may be reproduced in any form, or by any means, electronic or mechanical, including photocopying, recording, or any information browsing, storage, or retrieval system, without permission in writing from FriesenPress.

ISBN
978-1-03-910334-4 (Hardcover)
978-1-03-910333-7 (Paperback)
978-1-03-910335-1 (eBook)

1. FICTION, ACTION & ADVENTURE

Distributed to the trade by The Ingram Book Company

To Jack London who began it all by introducing the world to stories in which dogs were the central characters, replete with intelligence, spirituality and native cunning.

To C and E without whose enthusiastic support, ULYSSES would never have embarked on his epic journey.

To PM whose sensitive and perceptive editor's touch brought it all together and actually made it readable.

And to SED whose long-standing friendship, intelligence and belief turned it into a book.

CONTENTS

Chapter 1	'The Run'	1
Chapter 2	Ulysses is Missing	7
Chapter 3	The Journey to a Strange Land	13
Chapter 4	In the Beginning	19
Chapter 5	Max Pfister has a Problem	27
Chapter 6	The Search for Ulysses Continues	31
Chapter 7	Max and the Failed Experiment	35
Chapter 8	The Man in White	39
Chapter 9	The Crash	57
Chapter 10	The Aftermath	69
Chapter 11	Ulysses Begins his Journey	75
Chapter 12	Soleil Saves a Child	79
Chapter 13	The Race, The Storm	83
Chapter 14	Ulysses and the Giant Whirlpool	97
Chapter 15	Dimitri is Unhappy	103
Chapter 16	Mr. Yurei Gets an Assignment	107
Chapter 17	Ulysses Meets Some Unusual Companions	113
Chapter 18	The Truck	117
Chapter 19	The Mine	121
Chapter 20	The Rockslide	125
Chapter 21	Ulysses Reacquaints with a Friend	131
Chapter 22	The Kid	137
Chapter 23	The Kid Finds a Friend	145
Chapter 24	Ulysses's Unexpected Event	155
Chapter 25	Max's Surprise Encounter	161
Chapter 26	Ulysses is Rescued	167

Chapter 27	Max Pfister Finds a Benefactor	175
Chapter 28	Ulysses Needs Time to Heal	179
Chapter 29	Max Meets an Unwilling Ally	183
Chapter 30	Taking Stock	189
Chapter 31	Ulysses Meets an Adversary	195
Chapter 32	Luna says Good-bye	201
Chapter 33	Luna and Max Meet Again	203
Chapter 34	Ulysses Joins Luna and Max	213
Chapter 35	Max at the Crossroad	217
Chapter 36	Arriving Home	221
Chapter 37	Max Takes A Flight, and A Reunion	227
Epilogue		237
A song	"Following the Love"	238

CHAPTER 1

'THE RUN'

THERE ARE TWO GREAT ARCTIC DOG-TEAM RACES. THE BEST KNOWN is the Iditarod, 1,000 miles from Anchorage to Nome, Alaska, over 10 days. The most feared is simply referred to as *'The Run'* and it covers nearly 1,200 miles, starting just outside Fairbanks, Alaska, following part of the famous 1925 diphtheria serum dogsled relay south through Nenana to Eagle River then east across the border to Whitehorse in the Yukon territory. In the way, however, stand the Wrangell Mountains on the U.S. side of the border and Kluane National Park on the Canadian side, home to mountain peaks like Mount Queen Mary at 12,740 feet, and Mount Kennedy at 13,900.

Both races pay homage to the extraordinary events of 1925 when the city of Nome, Alaska was confronted with a deadly diphtheria outbreak. The only lifesaving serum was almost 700 miles away near the town of Nenana on the rail line just outside Anchorage. It had to get to Nome, and quickly. Almost overnight, a relay of 20 mushers and 150 dogs was assembled and the serum, insulated against the searing cold, began its perilous journey. Each team traveled between 30 and 40 miles, often in temperatures that plunged to minus 75 degrees Fahrenheit. The teams were thrashed by winds of hurricane force. Dogs died and mushers lost body parts. The most notable, seemingly impossible, feat was accomplished by 48-year-old Leonhard Seppala who, with his lead dogs Togo and Daisy, and a team of six Siberian Huskies, covered 261 miles, much of it on the shifting open ice of the Bering Strait. He passed off the serum with only 78 miles to go to Nome. Norwegian-born Gunnar Kaasen had the next leg and he headed into a vicious storm. Though totally blinded by the blizzard, his lead dog, Balto, managed to keep them on the trail. Crossing the open Bonanza Flat, the sled was flipped by the wind and its precious cargo disappeared into the night. Searching in the minus 40 degrees Fahrenheit darkness on his hands and knees, Kaasen was able to find the serum package and continue his journey. To this day, this remarkable lifesaving feat is known as the Great Race of Mercy.

This race aslo is known as The Killer because in the winter of 2001 an Arctic storm trapped six teams in an impassable blizzard. Eighty dogs and seven people died. They say the temperature plummeted to 70 below Fahrenheit for three days straight. They couldn't recover the bodies until the June thaw. 'The Run' requires the team and driver to navigate a virtually unmarked course for more than two weeks. Maps and GPS help, but the instincts and skills of the lead dog can make the difference between winning or losing and, sometimes, surviving.

Now in 2016, the greatest lead dog of them all was Ulysses, a five-year-old mixed-breed who weighed nearly 120 pounds. But he was not always the best. He led his first team in a race three years ago when he was only two years old and almost died because he, the team and driver, Dan McCord, became lost. Never mind that there was an eight-hour whiteout where trail markers and other competitors' tracks became invisible. His extraordinary instinct for direction should have helped when the GPS went down, but it didn't. A mining company helicopter found them and dropped supplies. They made it home. His owner, Dan McCord, thought about having Ulysses put down because what use is a lead dog who can't sense the position of the sun or tell north from south? Many of the other mushers assumed he would do just that after such a debacle. Once a lead dog, Ulysses could never wear any other harness. But that wasn't Dan's way. Sure, Ulysses could be used as a breeder, but it was the winning dogs whose semen brought in top dollar.

Most unusual of all was his appearance. He was pure white – as white as the snow he challenged like an enemy. No one could ever remember a white sled dog this big, not even Amos McTaggert and he's 97. Probably because he was so special-looking, he was allowed to live and when he raced the next year, he won. And he won again last year. This year he would race again and try to accomplish something that had never been done before – win '*The Run*' three times in a row. With a winner's prize of $100,000 and a bonus of $50,000 if Ulysses's team wins, the interest in this race was at an all-time high. It was the richest dogsled race in history. Even the television networks from the south sent up camera teams with announcers in oversized parkas from Abercrombie & Fitch. Dan McCord would say to anyone who would listen that next to the birth of his daughter, the two best things that ever happened to him were marrying Soleil and finding Ulysses. The dog had become so much more than just another sled dog that Dan would use in competition. Ulysses had formed a mysterious bond with Soleil and the baby and was even allowed to sleep at the foot of their bed in the log cabin Dan had built with his own hands.

The Start was in the town of Thompson, which boasted a summer population of 1,400. They said there were more than 4,000 people in town for the race this year. The 300 yards of snow-covered Main Street were lined with vehicles displaying out-of-state license plates, even one from Texas. Among the vehicles, a black and strangely clean pickup idled quietly in the lane beside Pettersen's Hardware. There was a festive atmosphere in Thompson and the two diners, the three bars, the hotel and the miner's hostel were doing booming business. 'The Run' was the best thing that ever happened to this town, and even Moody Jones, who began it 16 years ago and won the first race over only two other teams, couldn't have predicted its popularity today.

It got dark early in Thompson at that time of year – by the middle of the afternoon in fact. The few streetlights that worked came on at around 2:30, the stores and bars lit up a few minutes later, and by 4:00 the town looked and sounded like it did at midnight on the Fourth of July. It was filled with the boisterous sounds of people who don't often get to see other people. Jokes about "needing a little more anti-freeze," or, "having another internal alcohol rub – for safety reasons," and music, laughter and rough language were heard everywhere and spilled out onto Main Street. Big boots crunched on the gravelly snow. This was generally a happy, friendly crowd.

'The Run' was set to begin in two hours, at midnight on New Year's Eve. This wasn't a capricious or alcohol-fueled choice. It started at midnight so that when the teams arrived at The Gorge some 12 hours later, there would be light for them to navigate the first of many treacherous places on the route. The Gorge was well named, and a miscalculation near its precipitous edge would mean certain death for man and dog. A hundred yards from the start line, the 10 teams prepared. The air was filled with the yelping of over 120 impatient dogs. Harnesses were checked and dogs readied. Supplies and human food double-checked. Emergency Locator Beacons tested – mandatory equipment since the catastrophe of '01. The sled weighs over eight hundred pounds and that's only if the driver was running, not riding, and each dog will eat its own body weight in food before the race is over by burning 10,000 calories a day. The heaviest part of the load — food for the dogs; over 600 pounds of it — must be secured as close to the sled runners as possible. A low center of gravity is essential. And even then, eight hundred-pound sled traveling at 15 miles an hour could easily tip in a turn if the weight distribution wasn't perfect. A flip would be a threat to man and beast in an environment where injury has too often led to death. For this race, a stash of dog food at the halfway mark was permitted. Four hundred and fifty pounds of frozen meat was airdropped. Seal meat for its oil, and caribou for pure protein awaited the racers at a predetermined drop point. Each team was color coded, and no team ever touched another's supplies, even if they can't find their own.

Ulysses, as the lead dog would be the last into harness, and when that happened the other animals would settle. They know who was in charge. It wouldn't be the humans who would break up a fight among them, it would be Ulysses. His powerful presence had a calming effect. For now, he stood to one side, observing. Someone called out.

"Hey Dan, gimme a hand over here will ya?"

"Sure, Bernie."

Because Dan's team won last year, it will be Number One off the line this year. In a tradition as old as the race itself, all teams from 2 through 10 stood at the start ready to go, half on one side of the street, half on the other. The winning team from last year was the last to arrive and was paraded down Main Street accompanied by Innuit chanting and drumming. This evocative sound caused all the dogs to go silent, as if they recognized the presence of a strong spirit. The preparation compound was empty except for Ulysses, his team and the driver, Dan McCord. All the other dogs were waiting up at the Start, fidgeting, panting. Dan's magnificent white dog watched in the shadows from a distance, anticipating his time to move to the harness – the final act of preparation before the parade to the Start. He watched Dan check his sled again, testing the tie-downs, pulling on the canvas, giving the sled a hard shove this way and that. Dan was focused. Intense.

"Shit!" he said.

And to no one and everyone:

"This carabiner clip stripped its threads. How the hell did that happen? Gotta get over to Pettersen's."

Fortunately for Dan, the store was open until the start. He rushed off.

All of this was observed by a man concealed in the backdoor alcove of the Chinese restaurant. The shadow from a single light bulb concealed most of his face except for the trace of a smile crossing his lips. Mission accomplished. When Dan got back it would be time for Ulysses to take his position as the leader of the team.

Suddenly, Ulysses felt a sharp sting in his right hip. Even as his head spun around to see a shiny silver cylinder there, his legs began to feel weak. The streetlights started to darken. Then he was thrown into total darkness. A hood, a sack, something, covered him. It was tight around him. He yelped in pain. He was dragged. He felt the rough ground. He heard someone calling his name. He heard a smashing sound then silence except for the sound of the dragging. He was being dragged in the sack. Fast. Ulysses smelled a human he had never smelled before. The human smelled bad. Then he smelled smoke from a car. He was lifted; he was dropped. He heard a metal clang. He heard the zzipp-flapp of canvas being pulled. He smelled… what was it? Something sweet… something that made… him… feel… sick… dizzy… The last thing he felt was movement, and the last thing he heard was the distinctive sound of cold rubber crunching on 30-below snow.

CHAPTER 2

ULYSSES IS MISSING

DAN HELD HIS HEAD IN HIS HANDS TO STIFLE THE SOBS. HIS WIFE, Soleil, sat beside him doing her best to comfort him. She had never seen Dan like this. No one had. Despite her well-known skills as a Healer in both the First Nations and general population, there was nothing she could do for him. It was as if the Rock of Gibraltar had turned to chalk.

The two-officer Alaska State Trooper detachment in Thompson was small: two rooms, two desks, two computers, two landlines, a fax/printer and a bench along the opposite wall. The President and the Governor observed everything from their mass-produced portraits on the wall. Constable Emily Eagle had immediately called the Whitehorse and Yellowknife RCMP. An APB from them would carry more weight than one from a small town nobody outside Fairbanks had ever heard of. Nobody knew what to do. Ulysses had simply disappeared two minutes before the start of the race. No clues, no suspects. Everything was going exactly as it was supposed to – until it didn't anymore. Dan took a deep breath and reached out for the comfort of his daughter Akkisuktok, and hugged her. She was only five and very frightened because she had spent her entire life with Ulysses, and he was gone. To add to her distress, she had never seen her father like this.

The three of them sat on the bench, each lost in their own confused thoughts. Dan went over the events of two hours ago in minute detail one more time.

He remembered leaving Pettersen's Hardware and the stupid little bell over the door ringing as he rushed out, new $3 carabiner in hand. The blast of cold air reminded him that he had to be careful installing it as it would be warm from the store and his fingers might freeze to the metal. It was after all, minus 30 degrees. He remembered turning the corner onto Main Street and running to his sled. The music on the PA and the announcer filled the air as the start of the race was moments away. Dan bent to his task and switched out the broken piece of equipment. His dogs were getting restless, but he knew Ulysses's presence would calm them down. Over the PA, Dan heard the echoing call.

"And now ladies and gentlemen, mushers, dogs, marshals and fans, the moment we have all been waiting for!"

Someone cued up a brass fanfare to punctuate the announcer's call.

"Last year's winner – in fact the winning team from the last two years – Dan McCord and the magnificent Ulysses! Let's hear it for the Number One team this year! The team that will officially start this year's race in less than two minutes! You other nine teams, shake off those icicles and get ready." No one laughed.

Dan remembered turning to look for Ulysses where he had left him, quietly standing away from the sled and the dogs already in harness. He had been in the shadows, waiting. And Dan relived the sickening ache in the pit of his stomach when he realized Ulysses wasn't there. He knew instantly something was terribly wrong. He screamed at the top of his lungs.

"ULYSSES! ULYSSES!!"

His cries silenced the crowd nearby and several mushers ran toward him. He was on his knees in the snow, his head on the ground.

"He's gone. He was waiting right here 'cause he knew he had to be here, and then… he's gone."

Several of the crowd and mushers ran up the street and into the lanes between buildings, searching, all the time calling the dog's name. He remembered hearing a voice say, "Quick, call Deputy Eagle." And he remembered the music on the PA playing a jaunty tune. Dan remembered all that. And he felt the agonizing pain in his heart.

His reverie was interrupted by Deputy Eagle. Her concern for Dan was written on her face. She remembered Dan and his family from last year's race, and the image of his magnificent lead dog was etched in her mind. She remembered taking Akkisuktok and her mother to the airport in Fairbanks in her 4x4 to catch the last flight home when the bus wouldn't start. The deputy put her strong hand on Dan's shoulder.

"Dan, there's nothing more you can do here. Why don't you and your family go back to the hotel."

"Gotta look after my team. Strip their harnesses. Get them safe. I…"

"It's been done, Dan. Right after they started the race, Bernie McFadden took care of your dogs and your sled. They're all safe for tonight. Let me drive you to the hotel, the three of you."

Soleil squeezed his hand in gentle encouragement. Dan stood up feeling like there was something he should be doing. But he didn't know what. Exhaustion had set in. He couldn't think anymore. He couldn't feel anymore either, so he followed the others out to the 4x4 with the blue slash of Alaska highway painted on the door beside the familiar crest, mostly covered by winter's dust and snow, but still a reminder of a proud policing tradition stretching back to the beginning of statehood in 1959.

As the police vehicle made its way through the dark night, Akiss slept on her mother's lap and Dan, overcome with exhaustion, couldn't stop his head from falling onto Soleil's shoulder. She intertwined her arm with his and listened to his steady breathing. This was her family, and she felt a deep sense of purpose and pride at being at its center. Family. A profound and evocative word, equally powerful and meaningful in every language on Planet Earth. Everyone had a family of some kind or another. But Soleil did not always have a family in the traditional sense. She had foster parents, some good, some less so. She could remember only snapshots of her real family. Her mother's face with straight black hair framing it, always smiling. She remembered her mother's hair being so black it was almost deep, deep purple. And her father. Her dear Daddy, who was actually her stepfather, always tried hard to be stern, and usually failed. She never really understood what happened when they died. To spare the children, the social workers decided to tell them that their parents were sick and in a special hospital. It was a few years later that she heard from some kids at school that they had gone through the ice, through a fissure in the ice road, and that they were never found. So, when she was eleven, Soleil and her five-year-old sister were placed with a foster family in Yellowknife. They were nice people, she remembered, but they were European, from France; being Métis, she never felt she belonged. She knew her mother was Dene and that her stepfather was not. Her mother never spoke of Soleil's biological father other than that he was American.

It was six months after moving in with her foster parents that Soleil began the transition from girl to woman. And, simultaneously, she began to develop a remarkable sixth sense about people and their moods. They told her she had a high EQ – Empathy Quotient. She became curious about her cultural heritage and developed an interest in traditional medicine and the power of certain herbs, grasses and barks to heal a wide range of ailments. Soleil, a Métis herself, became involved with that community in Yellowknife and continued her studies. During the next three years she developed a reputation as a future Healer, and people sought her out. Her foster parents, though skeptical at first, soon realized that she possessed special abilities and they encouraged her but monitored her closely. She was, after all, only 15 years of age. They told her she had "a gift," and indeed she did. The family moved to Calgary when her stepfather pursued a new job. But it didn't work out. The oil business was not doing well, and even with some financial support from Social Services, they could not afford to keep the girls on.

Soon after, she and her sister found themselves in a new foster home, also in Calgary. The McIntyre family was Scottish Presbyterian and very strict. Soleil had only to endure the new environment for less than a year because when she turned eighteen, the foster home system was no longer obliged to support her. She was upset that she had to leave her sister, who was now 12, but she realized she had no choice. She did have a choice, however, of where to go, and she chose Yellowknife. Maybe there was some extended family there in the First Nations community. It would be a fresh start. And, she still had "her gift."

And she would meet the wonderful man whose heavy, curly red head was resting on her shoulder. She was only 19 at the time, but she knew in her heart and soul that Dan was the right man for her. They would create their own family. A real family in every sense of the word. Though aching with the loss of Ulysses, the purpose and pride she felt holding these two perfect people close made this dark, and fateful, night bearable.

CHAPTER 3

THE JOURNEY TO A STRANGE LAND

LATE IN THE AFTERNOON ON THE THIRD DAY AFTER ULYSSES'S DIS-appearance, the pickup turned into the parking lot behind a motel that overlooked Cannon Beach and the Pacific Ocean in northern Oregon. Under different circumstances, a visitor would notice Haystack Rock, a 245-foot high outcropping that was the only thing standing between the big rollers that started in Japan, and the hard sand shore. The driver got out, his long coat streaking the dusty fender. He dropped the tailgate. The sack that held Ulysses was opened – just a little – and the light stabbed his eyes. A tight, heavy leather collar was cinched around his neck and it hurt him. A chain was run through it and he was pulled out of the sack and onto the ground. He tried to stand but his legs wouldn't work, and he stumbled this way and that. He caught his first sight of the man. First the boots, then the hem of the coat, then the riding crop, then the hard face beneath the broad brim of the hat. Then Ulysses saw that one of the man's eyes was covered by a patch.

"You are some good-lookin' dog," said the man. "Even with all that shit on you. But you'll clean up 'cause I got plans for you."

He laughed. The man put a bowl of water down and poured some dry dog food onto the ground beside it. Awkwardly, Ulysses bent toward the food. He sniffed, suspicious, but his need overcame him, and he drank and ate and ate and drank. Slowly his legs stopped shaking and his strength returned. His nose smelled the salt in the air as he tested the wind, and his eyes focused on a solitary seagull soaring above. All the while the man just watched him.

A terrible anger welled up in Ulysses and with every ounce of his strength he lunged at the man, straight for his throat. Just when his teeth should have struck flesh, a head-snapping jerk stopped him inches short of his target. The man had carefully calculated exactly where to bolt the chain to the bed of the pickup, and where he should stand. The man laughed and Ulysses could smell the coffee on his breath as he strained against the chain.

"Good boy! Good boy!" said the man. "I knew you'd take a shot at me first chance you got. You got spirit, dog!"

His expression changed.

"Just no match for mine."

The riding crop in his right hand whistled through the air and caught Ulysses square across the snout – again and again and again. The pain was like nothing he had ever known. It seared through him like lightning through a tree trunk, and he fell back whimpering.

"Now back in the truck. You try that again and I'll hurt you more."

He grabbed the chain and pulled Ulysses back onto the pickup's flatbed where he secured a link to the side of the box.

"Tomorrow we'll be where I want to be. We'll get along OK, you and me, so long as you do it my way."

And he raised the riding crop once more. Ulysses didn't move an inch. His tongue tasted blood from the wound on his nose and his throat hurt from the collar, but he was like ice. Man and beast challenged each other with their eyes. The riding crop was raised again, and it whistled toward the dog's nose. But stopped short. Still Ulysses didn't flinch. The man tapped the hard leather against the dog's nose.

"So long as you do it my way."

The truck sped south along the open highway and, no longer in the canvas bag, Ulysses felt pleasure in the wind. The road brought to him visions of farming life and vehicles and people and animals. Animals. His animals. His sled mates. His humans and their child, now many days and nights away. An awful yearning crept into his heart. But the yearning was soon replaced by determination – a determination to return to them and to his home – somehow. He stood up and tested the chain. It was too strong. An effort at chewing on the metal quickly told him it was a hopeless task. He would have to wait.

The rain began in the middle of that afternoon. At first it was welcome as it cleaned the dried blood off his nose and washed the excrement from his coat. But as the man drove on into the night, the rain turned to snow as they gained altitude in the mountains. Though no stranger to snow and its cold, Ulysses suffered because he was exposed to the driving, chilling wind and the wet snow it hurled at him as they drove at 90 miles an hour. He had nowhere to go for protection. So, he curled into a ball like all sled dogs do and buried his nose between his paws. At least the air he breathed would be warm. And for the first time in four days, he slept. Maybe tomorrow his chance would come.

The following morning Ulysses was awakened by the sound of the truck stopping. They had pulled into a gas station with paint-faded pumps and an adjacent building that looked more like an unused garage than the Diner sign on its tired roof advertised. It was warmer now, and the rain was gone. The land was unlike anything he had ever seen. There were no trees, and the ground was brown instead of green or white, and there was nothing growing. The wind made dust rise up and it stung his eyes and nose. This was a strange land. Ulysses smelled meat cooking and his stomach stirred. He smelled the water in a pail beside the gas pump. He was so curious about his new surroundings that he didn't see the man approaching from behind. Swish! WHACK! and the riding crop smashed down on his snout again.

"That's for nothing, Boy. Just you see what happens if you try something!"

The pain in his snout was unbearable but he hid it behind soft brown eyes.

Soon…

The man pulled out his iPhone and tapped on the screen.

(text) *"Goods secured."*

(text reply) *"Proof of life."*

The man aimed his phone at Ulysses. *"Click"* and tapped the screen again. *"Whoosh."*

(text) *"Require second payment as agreed."*

Ulysses watched as the man stood silent.

"Ping"

(*text* reply) *"100,000 dollars transferred to your designated account."*

(text) *"Receipt acknowledged. Delivery details to follow."*

(text reply) *"You have 24 hours."*

(text) *"May require more time."*

The man stood silent again, waiting. Nothing. Finally, he dropped the phone back in his pocket and turned his attention to Ulysses.

"You're coming inside with me. Hell, if I leave you here, somebody might steal ya!"

He laughed as he unclipped the chain and gripped the leather collar. Ulysses could feel the man's strong fingers against the fur on his neck.

"Come on dog, get down outa there. I'm hungry."

And he gave the collar a hard pull in the direction of the diner. But Ulysses didn't jump down. He jumped up instead and caught the man full across the cheek with the claws of his left paw. Three deep gashes sprouted blood. The man screamed holding his hands to his face. Ulysses twisted free and the chain ran out through the buckle on the collar as he jumped down from the truck. He ran across the highway and into the scrub on the far side. Safely concealed, he turned and looked back. A woman in an apron had come out of the diner and was trying to help the man.

"Leave me alone! Leave me alone woman, goddamnit!" he screamed. "I don't need your help!"

The man looked across to where Ulysses was hiding, his good eye searching. He raised a fist into the air.

"I'm gonna get you dog! I'm gonna track you down and get you! No dog makes a fool outta Max Pfister!"

He watched the man splash water on his face from the bent pail beside the pump. Pale red liquid disappeared into the sandy ground. Ulysses watched quietly. A peace came over him. And then the stirring in his spirit began and he knew he had to start his journey, his odyssey. However long it took and whatever crossed his path, he knew his destiny was to return home to Dan and Soleil and the baby in the North. No matter where it would lead him.

And nothing would stop him.

CHAPTER 4

IN THE BEGINNING

FIVE YEARS EARLIER

SPRING CAME EARLY TO THE NORTH IN 2011. SOME SAID IT WAS climate change. It was late May in the Northwest Territories, and in these parts much of the ice was gone from the nearby lake. The streams that fed it were running fast and lively. There were still patches of snow in the forest at the base of the north-facing trunks of the larger trees where the warm spring sun had yet to penetrate. It was still too early for the few deciduous trees to release their new leaves but there were signs of fresh growth on the forest floor. Tiny white and blue scilla seemed impossibly fragile in this harsh domain but they were strong enough to break through the tangled earth and bark carpet to show their colorful petals to the animals and birds.

Dan McCord's cabin was feeling the influence of the change of season too. For the first time in seven months the snow was gone from his roof. The stove didn't need to be logged up all day and all night. His wife, Soleil, tended to the first of the spring-cleaning chores by doing a huge laundry and hanging it to dry on the line that ran from the outhouse to a linden tree. As the breeze nursed the sheets and towels dry, they seemed to make an endless series of happy waves to anyone, or anything, watching. The dogs in the nearby pens were barking a happy, noisy welcome to the new season.

Their baby, now almost six months, looked on from the snug comfort of her tikinagan (a cradleboard) that was hung from the cabin wall in such a way that she could watch her mother's every move as she went about her work. The baby was named Akkisuktok, which is Inuit for "Sunbeam," and she was born on the first day of the New Year in the Christian calendar, an event that pleased her father greatly. Because they had been locked in during the coldest time of the winter, Dan and Soleil had no choice but to birth the baby themselves. It was their first child and they were apprehensive, and though they felt well prepared, there was always the problem of what to do if something went wrong.

But on January 1, at 11:30 in the morning, following nine hours of labor, their daughter was born. Right after washing her eyes with a drop of silver nitrate and clearing her tiny nasal passages with what looked like a miniature turkey baster, Dan lifted the baby onto Soleil's wet chest and covered them both with a gray flannelette blanket. He dabbed the perspiration from her forehead and gently smoothed the wet hair away from her face. A few minutes later he cut and clamped the umbilical cord and washed Soleil with warm sterile towels. He then cleared away the placenta, whose rich chemistry would nourish the dogs.

When he came back, the Arctic sun had found the small east-facing window and a sliver of light not more than two inches wide lay streaked across the bed. It lit up the room and both he and Soleil felt that that something special and spiritual had just happened. Soleil reached for Dan's hand and squeezed it tight. He was surprised that she had such strength left, and he lifted her hand to his lips and kissed it.

"Akkisuktok," she said.

"I'm sorry. What?"

"Akkisuktok," she repeated. "It's Inuktitut for what the English call a sunbeam. It also means 'little sun' for those times when the sun is small in the sky but still has a big influence on the people below."

"Then let's name her Akkisuktok," Dan said. "'Akkis' for short, like in 'A kiss.'"

And so they did.

Gradually, winter loosened its grip on Dan and his family. And gradually, Soleil regained her strength. The baby thrived and doubled her weight in the first three months. As soon as spring arrived, they would introduce her to the world outside the four walls of the cabin. They would watch as her bright blue eyes widened at the sight of a bird landing on the clothesline or squinting when the sunlight became too strong. They knew she was smelling the bucolic musk of the forest and turning her head to see where the smoke smell was coming from. She reacted to the sounds of the dogs a short distance away. The flap-flap of the washing on the line caught her attention, too. As did the North's workhorse de Havilland Beaver 2,000 feet overhead with its 9-cylinder radial engine barking at the sky.

Dan rested his shovel beside the door and wiped his face.

"It might be warming up but the ground's still pretty hard. I was trying to dig a new pit for the privy but I'm afraid we'll have to wait a little longer."

Soleil looked up from the logs she was stacking.

"Don't worry, one of us is still in diapers for a while yet."

They hugged each other and a silence fell about them.

"Yeah, I miss her too," Dan whispered.

Soleil pulled back slightly and raised an eyebrow.

"Were you really thinking about Sheba at exactly that moment?"

"I was actually thinking what an almost perfect moment this is except there's someone missing."

Soleil returned to his arms and hugged him an extra-long hug.

"I don't know why she left," she said into his chest, "and it made me sad too, especially not knowing if she was alive or…"

"Many animals become feral when they are preparing to give birth," Dan said. "She had to leave because, well, because she had to."

Dan went over to the tikinagan and unhooked it from the peg. He cradled the baby and her carrier in his arms.

"Whoa! Somebody needs changing!"

Akkisuktok cooed in agreement and broke into a gummy smile. Soleil looked up from her work.

"I'll be done in a few minutes. Would you put a good-sized log into the stove please? I'll start dinner soon."

It always amazed Dan how Soleil could cook such interesting meals. Much of their diet was made up of dehydrated foods but that never stopped her magic at the stove. They had just finished a dinner of chicken stew, mashed potatoes and lentils, with apple-and-cranberry sauce for dessert, all washed down with lapsang souchong tea. The smoky aftertaste was the perfect prelude to the finale – an ounce each of their precious Laphroaig Single Malt, also with a smoky essence, created in a very different part of the world. They had rationed their single bottle to last through the winter, poured two small glasses, and there remained one last exquisite ounce.

With the baby swaddled and asleep in their bed, they watched through the slats in the cast iron door of the stove as the flames danced inside in a sort of voyeuristic striptease. A Procol Harum CD played quietly. With their scotch in one hand and each other's hand in the other, they were filled with love. Soleil took the last sip of her drink and leaned over and kissed Dan, and then kissed him some more.

"Hold on there, you impatient woman. You're going to make me spill my scotch!"

Never taking her eyes from his she slipped the glass from his hand and put it on the small table beside the big chair.

"Hey, I'm not finished with that."

"You are for now…"

"Hold it," Dan said suddenly. "Did you hear that?"

"Hear what?"

"Scratching. That scratching."

Their passion distracted, they listened. Sure enough, there was a sound at the door to the cabin. A scratch? A whimper?

"Stay here, Dan. It's just a critter."

"No. No, it's not."

Dan took the three long strides to the door and opened it.

"Oh my God! Soleil, come quick!"

There, closer to death than to life, lay Sheba, panting. The first thing they saw were three terrible gashes on her side. Most of the skin was peeled back and her ribs were white and bloody. Part of her intestine was spilling from her body. The next thing they saw was the puppy she had carried by the scruff of its neck until she collapsed at the cabin door. It was only two or three days old and barely alive. Its still-shut eyes had protected it from seeing what was likely a bear that had killed the other four in the litter and damaged the mother almost beyond belief.

"Sheba! Oh, Sheba. Oh my God," wailed Soleil.

"Here, take the puppy." Dan handed her the half-dead animal.

Sheba raised her head as if to protest but the effort was too much and she fell back, her breath raspy. Dan looked down at the once beautiful sled dog which he and Soleil had raised from a pup. Of all their dogs, she had been their favorite and they allowed her to sleep at the foot of their bed. Anger shook him as he looked at her broken body and he cursed the cruelty of nature. He went back into the cabin. Tears filled Soleil's eyes as she watched him take his new C-19 bolt-action rifle from the rack over the door, its stainless-steel barrel catching the light from the fire. He slid the bolt back to confirm that there was a bullet in the chamber, slammed it shut and slung the rifle over his shoulder. He knelt and picked up the dog in his arms with all the tenderness he could find.

"Try to feed the puppy, will you? It may be too late."

As he left, Soleil cradled it to her breast and felt its shallow, labored breathing. With a warm, damp cloth she wiped as much of the blood off it as she could. There were no obvious injuries. She buried her nose in its pale fur and smelled the still-sweet newness of birth. She made a soft nest on the floor in front of the stove with a well-used gray flannelette blanket, and gently tucked the puppy into it. Soleil then went to the kitchen and, hiking up her sweater, expressed some of her milk into one of the baby's bottles. She screwed the top down and retrieved the animal from its warm place. She sat in the bentwood rocker just as she did every day with Akkis and encouraged the pup to take the rubber nipple. At first it didn't respond but when a single drop of milk touched its mouth, a tiny pink tongue reached out to seek more of the warm, welcome liquid. Soleil rocked back and forth rhythmically. Much of the milk stained the blanket but some of it went where it was intended to go. The bottle empty, the tiny animal took a deep shuddery breath and fell asleep.

Soleil could hear the excited barking of the dogs as Dan walked toward the pens. But then suddenly they went silent, and she wondered if many of them recognized their mortally wounded mother in his arms. She held her breath. A single gunshot echoed through the woods as if announcing a death again and again and again. Soleil slumped back into her chair. Her attention returned to the tiny ball hanging on to life in her lap. She caressed its damp fur and rubbed it between the ears. They would know by the morning whether it would live or die. There was nothing more they could do now, so she returned the sleeping animal to its nest by the stove. Soleil retrieved the bottle of Laphroaig and poured the remainder of its contents into Dan's glass.

And waited for him to return on this terrible evening in May when the Spring came early.

CHAPTER 5

MAX PFISTER HAS A PROBLEM

PRESENT DAY

MAX STARED INTO THE BLACK COFFEE AT THE GYRATING REFLECtion of the florescent light. In the diner's washroom he had applied antiseptic cream to his cheek and covered it with a gauze pad and tape. It hurt like hell but that was not what was bothering him. That was only pain and it would go way. His other problem wouldn't. The first $100,000 had been spent. The new truck, the travel and a deposit on the lab at UC Davis, had eaten up a lot of it. The rest had gone to the remaining debts in closing up Good Grace Airlines, and the last of his hospital bills, still unpaid and being pursued after five years.

"Fucking insurance companies."

"Sorry dearie. Did you want to order something else?"

Max's silent look gave her the answer.

Now he had the second $100,000 in his bank account, no dog, and a very powerful client, who will be very pissed off if he finds out.

So, get smart, Max, he thought to himself. *Analyze the situation. No emotion. This needs logical, intelligent analysis, that's all.*

His whole wheat toast with honey arrived. The woman with the apron looked at him but mercifully said nothing. Max didn't need people bothering him right now. He was in a black mood and in a predicament, and he couldn't see his way out of it. Max found himself in a very different time and place now, and he didn't like any of it. Until half an hour ago everything had gone exactly to his carefully worked-out plan, right down to the detail of which roads he would take and which towns he would avoid on his trip south. It was foolproof until that goddamn sneaky dog…

The gas station diner was near Jackson, CA., which boasted a population of 4,651, and was only 45 miles from the lab at UC Davis just outside Sacramento. He had driven south on Route 49, which runs along the western boundary of Yosemite National Park, part of his plan to stay off main Interstates in the U.S. and major highways in Canada on his journey south from Fairbanks. Although he was fairly certain he had well concealed his truck before the start of the race, and no one in Thompson had seen it or him, he had to be careful. He knew there was an alert out. The race people would have notified the Alaska State Patrol and maybe the Mounties. But he doubted they would have contacted the FBI. It was just a stolen dog after all. Still, he had to be careful. According to Google Maps, the drive south from Fairbanks to this location should have taken around 45 hours and he needed to be away from there as fast as possible. Five hours after leaving Thompson, Alaska, he entered Yukon, Canada. His research had shown that the station at the Alcan-Beaver Creek Border Crossing was open 24 hours. He also knew that the border guards usually inspected RVs with great care. In case they might ask him to open the cover of his pickup, he had moved the still-sedated Ulysses onto the floor of the back seat, still in his canvas prison, and covered him with his coat. He showed the officer his University of California ID and his California driver's license. He was waved thorough without incident. It was after all, 5:30 in the morning. With snow on the road he had to manage his speed, and it wasn't until he crossed the 60th parallel just south of Watson

Lake and into British Columbia, that he could start to make some time. He drove for 16 hours straight on the first leg. His GPS told him that the route through Prince George was the shortest. And, he hoped, just after the New Year's holiday, there would be less traffic on the road. And that would mean fewer cops. He made it to this gas station in Jackson, California, in 39 hours, a journey of almost 2,400 miles. And his precious cargo was healthy – if you didn't count the cuts on his nose.

He threw a $5 bill on the table and returned to his truck, still at the pumps. He slammed the tailgate shut and pulled the tarp over the cargo space, now empty except for a large, flat canvas sack.

"I need a place to think. Think. Think."

The GPS showed a small airport just outside Jackson, a three-mile drive to the northwest. Max always found that aircraft spoke to his soul, and whether in them or around them, they brought him tranquility and a clarity of mind. He wheeled onto Route 49 and hit the gas. Twenty minutes later he pulled into the dusty single strip airport. The black runway was numbered 1-19, which reflected the compass setting for the prevailing winds. There was a small two-storey building beside the aircraft parking area bearing the sign: "Elev. 1,690 ft," signifying this was the control tower — such as it was. A single Cessna 150 was in the circuit doing touch-and-goes. A student most likely. "Lucky bastard," he said under his breath.

Max parked his truck in the shade of the building, left the engine idling and kicked up the AC a notch. To the mechanic passing by he just looked like a man sleeping in his truck. But whatever is at the other end of the spectrum from sleeping is where Max's mind was working. Like a computer-generated animation, dozens of images flashed through his brain, each for no longer than a heartbeat. White dog, road sign, river, blood, dog sled, black truck, chain, open snow-covered highway, gas pump, Motel sign, night, dawn, road sign, white dog – then the face of the man who would probably kill him. He caught his breath and sat bolt upright. Max's heart was beating fast. His spontaneous visceral reaction to this possibility surprised and terrified him. It wasn't dying that Max was afraid of. It was the act of dying. In the world inhabited by, and indeed controlled by, his client, the baser the act the better seemed to be the law of that jungle. The little Cessna took three bounces on the runway before the young pilot reapplied the power, earned some altitude, and rejoined the circuit. Max had to force his mind back to the dog and get inside Ulysses's mind. He had studied a lot about canine behavior, instincts, genetics, socialization. He knew two things for sure. Ulysses would head north and begin the seemingly impossible journey back to the Arctic. And he also knew that the animal would travel close to a source of water. He took an iPad from the glove box and powered it up. He sourced a topographical map of the area with roads superimposed. He studied the image for a full five minutes in silence swiping back and forth, up and down.

"Of course!" he muttered. "That's where you're going." He closed the iPad.

"And I'm going to be there to meet you."

CHAPTER 6

THE SEARCH FOR ULYSSES CONTINUES

DAN MCCORD RECOVERED. CARING FOR SOLEIL AND AKKISUKTOK IN their small cabin in the woods in the grip of the northern winter was a full-time job, and he had his dogs to tend to daily. Twelve dogs took some caring for. And when two of them came into heat in the spring and were bred, his job would become even more challenging. Dan had a reputation in the North for breeding strong, good-tempered dogs who never got into fights in harness. And having won 'The Run' for the last two years and the $50,000 in prize money each year, he had a well-run operation and his dogs brought in a good price. With Ulysses as the lead dog, Dan and his team were the ones to beat. During the summer he had all the carpentry work he wanted. He wasn't the fastest in the Territory perhaps, but his workmanship was matchless. Six years ago, when he began his breeding business, he moved out of the family home in Yellowknife and built this cabin. The cabin was snug enough and safe enough but surviving in the North meant never taking nature for granted. A blizzard depositing six feet of snow had to be prepared for; a drop in temperature to minus 50 degrees Fahrenheit had to be expected. The time for feeling sorry for himself and the loss of his magnificent Ulysses was over. He knew he had been poor company for Soleil, and he loved her deeply for her willingness to love him and support him despite his distant behaviour. He had been remote with her but had tried not to let his pain show to Akkis. Of the three of them, she was the most open with her feelings of loss, and tears frequently overwhelmed her. The three of them would sit by the fire, Akkis cuddled in the middle, and watch the wiggly television signal – on a good evening. Without warning, she would sniffle, then begin to sob quietly. Soleil would have her lie in her lap, and she stroked the little, unhappy girl's hair with a touch the weight of a rose petal. She looked up at her mother. She had inherited her blue eyes from her father. Given the Native tone of her complexion and her obsidian hair, the result was a little girl with a powerful look about her. She sat up and faced her mother.

"Why, Mommy. Why did Ulysses go away?"

"We've talked about this before, and the answer is still the same. We just don't know."

"Doesn't Ulysses love us anymore?"

"My darling, Ulysses will always love us, and we will always love him."

Soleil remembered that fateful night five years ago when Sheba, on the precipice of death, had collapsed on their doorstep carrying a three-day-old pup in her mouth. By good fortune and the beautiful nourishment of her milk, the animal had not only survived but had grown into an extraordinary adult sled dog, the likes of which had never been seen in the North before. Dan and Soleil thought long and hard when selecting a name, and they chose Ulysses because of the incredible journey against all odds that he and his mother, Sheba, had taken to get to their cabin and into their lives. For the first six months of his life (the second six months of Akkis's life), the puppy lived in his flannelette nest close to the stove. When Soleil brought Akkis to her breast she would bottle-feed

Ulysses at the same time. The two fragile little creatures thrived on the same diet. This routine created a triumvirate of spirits that would be connected in an almost mystical way. Soon Akkis outgrew her tikinagan and began to sleep between her mother and father. At the same time, Ulysses always found a place at the foot of the bed.

"But if he loves us why did he leave us? You and Daddy would never do that, would you?"

Her wide eyes asking questions impossible to answer. Soleil hugged her, perhaps a little too tightly.

"No sweetheart, of course not. We will always be here for you and we will always love you. And you know what else?"

"What?"

"I know deep in my heart that Ulysses will come back. He will come home to us. We don't know where he is, but whatever we are feeling for him, however much we miss him and love him, he is feeling the same way. I know he misses you with all his heart, and somehow we will all be together again."

"When?"

"As soon as it can possibly be. We must always send our love out to him to guide him and help him find his way home. Love is a powerful force and a strong messenger."

Dan finished his coffee and joined the conversation.

"And you know what also?

"What, Daddy?"

"While Ulysses is looking for us, we are going to be out looking for him! What do you think of that?"

"Cool. What are we going to do?"

Dan explained that he had contacted the Alaska State Troopers and the RCMP in Yellowknife to be sure they were still on the case. They had assured him they were; the RCMP reported that they had sent out another notice to their detachments in the three Western provinces in Canada, and a separate alert to the police in Yukon. But they had nothing to report yet. Although winter roads and long nights made driving at this time of year difficult and dangerous, Dan told them that every day he would drive a different road for at least 50 miles, stopping at every gas station, diner, general store or business to leave a poster with a picture of Ulysses, and their phone number. He had also contacted the Sled-dog Owner's Association and they had placed a notice on their Facebook page. And, he had sent an email to every veterinarian within two hundred miles to be on the lookout. Dan knew that Ulysses had not just wandered off. He knew someone had taken him. Who, and why, and to where, were the mighty questions for which there were no answers.

Akkis had fallen asleep in her mother's arms so Soleil tucked her under the covers and snugged the blanket under her chin. She looked at Dan who returned her gaze. They both knew something dreadful had happened to Ulysses and that his life was probably in danger. Also possible was that they might never see him again – but neither felt able to put that unthinkable thought into words. Soleil shifted her position slightly, folded her hands in her lap and dropped her chin onto her chest. She began to breathe deeply and rhythmically, and soon drifted into that meditative state where she communicated with her ancestors, with her spirit guide, with her soul, and yes, with Ulysses.

CHAPTER 7

MAX AND THE FAILED EXPERIMENT

THE SCHOOL OF VETERINARY MEDICINE AT THE UNIVERSITY OF California, Davis campus, is located in an architecturally unremarkable building, two stories high with tall windows situated in a white, Mansard-style wall-roof. Whatever world-class work was being done within the walls, and it was, the same could not be said for the building itself. There had been a clamor at the time for a structure with a more progressive design, more imaginative, more... "contemporary California academia." But because no one could figure out what that term actually meant, and because the state budget was obscenely tight, the contract went to the lowest bidder who, predictably, showed the least imagination. Behind the third tall window, counting from the entrance, was one of the many offices occupied by the staff. The window offices were reserved for professors and researchers with the greatest number of degrees or publications, no matter how arcane, behind their names. More modestly labeled academics occupied the inner offices.

So it was that one of these offices was occupied, albeit temporarily and pro bono, by Dr. Max Pfister, MD, PhD in canine genetics and a Masters in Medieval History and Fine Art. His PhD thesis, "Super Dog – Genetic Planning to the Perfect Canine," was brilliant and caused quite a stir internationally. But like much in academia, it came and went and was soon forgotten. In equal measure to the intelligence of Dr. Pfister was his complete lack of likeability. He operated in a world of his own in which there was only room for polymaths and geniuses like himself. That was his view of the world; and in his view, the only possible view. Respected for his brilliance, he was equally disliked for his lack of social graces and his inability to engage with fellow human beings without insulting them or making them feel inferior. Theories abounded on campus as to why he was so socially inept. His flaws were far more profound than simple bad manners. Perhaps it had something to do with the plane crash that cost him his eye, or the fact that the Medical Board of California had suspended his license because he practiced only on animals. Whatever it was, it had left behind a profoundly flawed and bitter person. That noted, the major pet food companies admired his work and were major donors to UC Davis.

On this particular day, Max was on a video call to Juneau, Alaska, where his home and his sled-dog breeding business were located. There were two young assistants at the other end of the call huddled together in front of the laptop camera. Max's voice was quiet, modulated and created the same effect on the listener as if standing barefoot on the ice currently covering most of Juneau Harbor.

"I don't give a good goddamn what the vet up there said, I'm telling you that based on the Day 1 birth photos you sent me, and the Day 2 follow-ups, the whole litter is a disaster!"

"But Dr. Pfister, I..."

"Shut up and listen. That litter is history. I want it destroyed. I DO NOT breed dogs that look like that. That kind of anomaly is an insult to my profession and to me personally. Get it done. Am I clear on that?"

"Yes, sir. But..."

"No buts. Put them in the freezer. The lot of them. Am I clear?"

"Yes, doctor. We understand."

'*Click.*' Max broke the connection. The boys in Juneau were capable enough, but in his view, following the instructions of your superior is job one. Maybe their attitude had something to do with having Native blood. Whatever the reason he would set them straight next time he went North. Besides, euthanizing puppies by freezing them to death was actually humane. He considered himself a compassionate man after all. What was the problem?

He sat for a full ten minutes staring at a spot in space trying to figure out what had gone wrong with that breeding. The gene profiles of both the dam and the sire were just what he wanted them to be. And yet the entire litter was born with dark spots on their beige fur. Unacceptable. His animals not only were the best, but they looked the best. You could tell a Max Pfister sled dog half a mile away. Size, build, color. And no goddam spots. Two months wasted. Things were tough enough without this. Goddam it!

"How dare they do that to me!" he said to no one in particular.

CHAPTER 8

THE MAN IN WHITE

NO SOONER HAD HE HUNG IT UP, THE TELEPHONE RANG.

"What NOW?!"

Without introduction or pleasantries, a voice spoke.

"Bernard Smote."

Max's blood ran cold. This man was powerful, cold and calculating, and Max was in his debt. He said nothing and waited. As did Bernard Smote. For Max, the silence was sickening. For Smote, effective. He had Max on the defensive. He continued in his cultured, slightly accented voice.

"Without dwelling on your two previous failures, I have a business proposal to offer to you. Since the last time we met two years ago, I have established a new location, a necessary requirement from time-to-time in my profession. I will have a car outside the main entrance of the Veterinary Studies Building, where I believe you are currently situated, in 30 minutes."

The phone went dead. Max looked at the telephone as if to find an answer there to what had just transpired. He sat down heavily in his chair and waited for his heart rate to return to normal. He detested this man but feared him more. Max took a deep breath and dabbed at his damp forehead with a white cotton handkerchief, looking this way and that to make sure nobody noticed.

Bernard Smote had approached Max three years ago, introducing himself as a dealer in art, artifacts and exotic animals. He had heard about a young and remarkable white sled dog and had a foreign client who was looking for just such an animal. He knew of Max's reputation as a successful sled-dog and medical-specimen dog breeder who knew animals as well as all the breeders in the North. This two-year-old animal was located in Yellowknife, reasonably easy access from Juneau where Max lived and had his breeding operation. Max had, in fact, heard of this dog too, and that he was owned by a breeder named Dan McCord. He figured he would have no difficulty convincing this north country hick to part with the dog. All he had to do was wave money under his nose. He would sell. Smote had offered Max $5,000 (plus expenses) plus 10% of the sale price, to buy the dog, sedate it, crate it for travel, prepare the necessary documentation, and ship it south on Alaska Airlines. Max accepted the job and the money and flew to Yellowknife.

He failed. McCord simply wouldn't sell. No way. Whether it was because he and the dog had just barely survived a terrible storm that had killed his father, or some other reason, McCord was adamant. No sale. It was then that Max's relationship with Bernard Smote turned dark. Smote reimbursed Max for his flight and hotel, then demanded the fee be returned. Problem was, Max had spent it, being confident he could get McCord to sell.

"What do you mean you don't have the money?" The voice on the phone demanded.

"Mr. Smote, I was so sure McCord would sell that I, well, I spent the fee on 'other items.'"

The IRS was being very insistent. There was silence at the other end of the call. It was more than icy, it was close to Absolute Zero, a temperature at which no living creature can survive. Max waited.

"Dr. Pfister, this is unfortunate. Very unfortunate indeed. Although I am not unaware of your general financial circumstances, I cannot let this go unresolved. I consider this an unpaid debt and will take steps to resolve the issue."

And that is the way it was left, just hanging there agonizingly, until a year later when Smote contacted Max again.

"Dr. Pfister. I will give you an opportunity to settle your debt with me. The dog we discussed last year, I understand his name is Ulysses, won '*The Run*' last week as a three-year-old. The client we both disappointed last year remains interested in acquiring this animal. So, I propose you approach this McCord man again and convince him to sell. You are authorized to offer him up to $50,000 for the animal. You will be paid a commission of 10%, from which your debt will be deducted. How you finance your journey to Yellowknife is your affair not mine. Do you agree?"

Max swallowed hard. He really had no choice. So, a week later, he met with Dan McCord again, but no amount of discussion, persuasion, pressure or veiled threat would change the man's mind. Ulysses was simply not for sale at any price. Max could not reach Smote by phone to tell him of his lack of success, and the man refused to acknowledge his emails. It was almost as if he already knew. The matter between Max and Bernard Smote went into limbo again.

Smote's call this morning came as a complete surprise and Max had no choice but to accept his 'invitation.' Max was somewhat comforted by the fact they were still talking. He was very curious to know what Bernard Smote was going to propose. Whatever it was, he just had to get this monkey off his back. Exactly 30 minutes later, a white limousine pulled up at the front entrance of his building. It was a Mercedes 600 Series long wheelbase, a model favored by diplomats and drug lords. He reached for the rear handle and was surprised to find the door unusually heavy. As he entered the car the door closed slowly behind him on its own, with a firm thud/click. This was an armoured vehicle and the darkness of the window glass reinforced the observation. Max settled into the rich white leather seat as the car accelerated silently away. He could only see the driver's head and shoulders, and he appeared to be a large man. Other than a quick glance into the rearview mirror he did nothing to acknowledge the presence of his passenger. There was chilled bottled water and a Waterford crystal glass in a tray beside his seat, and a copy of the *San Francisco Chronicle* in the unoccupied seat. As he had no idea where he was being taken, he decided to watch the road signs and keep his bearings as best he could.

The car was traveling on I-80 South through the towns of Rodeo, El Sobrante, Vacaville and Richmond, which told him they were going in the general direction of San Francisco, usually an hour-long drive from UC Davis. The road changed to I-580 and a sign indicated that Berkeley was not far away. The car slowed, took an off-ramp and was soon on a narrow residential street with large, but nondescript, houses along one side, empty land on the other. Max could see no street name. The car turned to face a double garage door. Max could see no number. The door opened to admit the large vehicle into an empty garage. The door closed behind them. Max heard a quiet click and his passenger door slowly swung open.

Standing there was a Japanese man of perhaps 60 years, black hair graying at the temples and perfect posture. He was wearing a carefully tailored blue rough silk jacket buttoned up to its Nehru collar, with pants to match. On his feet were a pair of dark blue brocade slippers. He offered a deep bow of greeting.

"I am Hisa. Welcome."

And he beckoned Max to follow him. Strangely, this was the first time Max and Mr. Smote had met face-to-face. The top of the stairs opened into a large, airy and unusual room. Hisa stepped aside. One wall was all window and looked out on to a treed park. Two joggers challenged the narrow gravel path. Max scanned the room quickly. Something wasn't quite right. It took him a moment to realize that the room was almost devoid of furniture. It was more like a gallery or a museum. Several pictures were carefully hung to avoid direct sunlight, and one or two looked familiar. Another was covered with a green cloth. There were many ceramics, plates and pots on display, but it was a Chinese porcelain vase about 28 inches high standing on a plexiglass display block that caught his attention. But what dominated this curious room was the aquarium. At about 8 feet long, 6 feet high and 4 feet wide, it was by far the largest domestic aquarium he had ever seen. He estimated it contained well over 200 gallons of water. And in it were two large, slender silvery fish whose most notable characteristics were two long feathery fins, one running from mid-belly to tail along the belly, and another down their back. The fins rippled to propel the fish through the water. And the fish were large. Each specimen was close to three feet in length.

"They are carnivores, you know. Freshwater carnivores. These two are just full grown."

Max turned to see a man a head shorter than himself, slightly overweight and probably around his age of 47. He had a way about him that was not as much effeminate as it was effete. He had a pale indoor-looking complexion, very close-cropped salt-and-pepper hair, and strong clear-blue eyes. Most noticeable was that he was dressed entirely in white – including white cotton gloves. *Possibly a germaphobe,* Max thought to himself. He extended his hand.

"We finally meet. I am Max Pfister."

The two stood in silence, each taking the measure of the other. The man looked at Max without apparent emotion and made no effort to accept his gesture. Instead, he walked over to the massive tank putting about six feet of distance between them. The two men gazed at the graceful fish whose silvery white scales were almost translucent.

"The Platinum Arowana – *Osteoglossum bicirrhosum*. When I acquired these two about a year ago, they were half the size. And half the price. A collector in Hamburg has made an offer which I will probably accept. He wanted full grown specimens."

Max listed patiently wondering where this was going and when he would get to the point.

"Do you know anything about collector fish, Dr. Pfister?"

"I do not."

"Then you will undoubtedly be interested to learn that these specimens will sell for close to $400,000 each. The buyer is proposing a discount for the pair. Seems a reasonable request, don't you agree?"

Max nodded slightly and began to feel impatience creeping into his mood.

"But I didn't invite you here to discuss fish, now did I."

Max nodded again. Smote continued.

"Our previous disagreement aside for the time being, I know you are a man of sophistication, Dr. Pfister. As well as being familiar with your skills in the world of dog- breeding and husbandry, I have read the paper you wrote on the study you did for your Master's degree on "Statuary of the Italian Renaissance and Oriental Pottery of the Same Period."

Max was impressed, and more than a little unnerved, by how much research this man had done into his background. His host continued.

"Please allow me to show you an item of which I am particularly fond. Then we will discuss our business."

He led Max to a wall opposite the aquarium on which hung the picture covered by a piece of green silk.

"Would you like some tea?"

"Thank you, yes."

"Hisa, will you bring tea for our guest and the usual for me, please."

Hisa bowed and left the room silently. Smote returned his attention to the draped picture.

"I keep it covered to protect it from the light. It's rather fragile."

He removed the covering and Max gasped. He couldn't help it.

"Apparently you know this work."

Max let his eye take in every detail of the painting. It was extraordinary. It showed a princely looking young man with dark brown hair cascading over his right shoulder, a white blouse and a cape or a jacket over the other shoulder. The figure was seated and looking at the artist just to his left. He had wide, curious eyes, a strong but not quite aquiline nose. and sensual lips over which the barest trace of a smile was playing. His right elbow was resting on something unseen, causing his hand to fall languidly. The entire effect was of relaxed masculine sensuality.

Max let out his breath as if he had been holding it for a long time. Which in fact he had.

"This is extraordinary!" was all he could manage to say.

Max collected himself and continued.

"Raphael's 'Portrait of a Young Man!' Painted very early in the 16th century.

"Correct," said Smote. "It is generally dated to around 1510. Hence my concern for it being exposed to light."

Max continued to look on the treasure before him with amazement. He carried on.

"As I recall, the Gestapo seized it early in the war and it became part of the Führermuseum in Linz," Max said. "This piece was last seen at the end of the Second World War, was it not?"

"Correct again. In Krakow, in the Wawel Castle to be precise. And then it disappeared."

Max, his pulse rate returning to normal, turned to face the man in white.

"May I ask where you acquired it?"

"You may not."

"Through a dealer?"

"I did. But let's just say it wasn't Christie's or Sotheby's and leave it at that, shall we Dr. Pfister? Obviously, the great challenge with a piece like this is how to return it to civilization. And realize a reasonable financial gain in the process. One cannot simply walk into the Louvre or the Tate with it under one's arm, now can one? No, one must be a good deal more… imaginative.

"Something tells me you have a plan."

Hisa arrived with Max's tea and a glass of milk for his host. The tea was served in an exquisite Chinese porcelain cup, white with classic cobalt blue painting, no handle. Max rested the cup on the white cotton napkin in his other hand and raised it to is nose. Bernard Smote picked up his milk from the ebony tray, took a half step toward Max and fixed him with his gaze.

"I can tell you this much. A gentleman in Rome took an option on this painting. He paid five million euros for me to hold it for him with a guarantee it would not be transacted until a year has passed."

"And what is he going to do?"

"I don't know, and I couldn't tell you if I did. But suffice it to say that several years ago, I had a Tiepolo of, shall I say, 'uncertain provenance.' Another client was interested in it, so he purchased an ancient monastery outside Siena. No one could understand why he would spend money on a building in such terrible condition. But he did and immediately began renovating the place. Well, what do you think he found when he took up the floorboards on the second floor?"

Max smiled at the simplicity of it.

"And because it 'came with the property,' and because the Tiepolo had not been reported stolen – at least nothing recorded in the 20th century – he could claim legitimate ownership and put it up for auction."

"And is that what will happen to the Raphael?"

"Something like that, I expect. My buyer had 12 months to devise an interesting and credible way to 'discover' the Raphael and has, apparently, accomplished that."

Mr. Smote gazed at the picture of the refined courtier for a long time.

"These are my last days with this beautiful young man. He will leave here shortly for his new home in… well, let's just say it's not in California. The picture will go to auction, the proceeds of which will be shared one third by me and two thirds by my client. So, given that it could get knocked down for fifty or sixty million euros, we would both be satisfied."

Max gazed at the remarkable painting again, afraid he would miss some detail of this masterpiece he would likely never see again.

"I believe there is a flaw in your plan – or rather, your client's plan."

"You are quite correct. But the risk is his, not mine."

Max continued, enjoying the repartee.

"Once the painting is 'discovered,' what if a claim is made on it by the heirs or the estate of the original owners? They were Polish, were they not?"

"Correct again. You know your art history, Dr. Pfister."

"A little. I took a Masters in Medieval History."

"And Fine Art. Yes, I know."

There was an eloquent pause as both men sipped their beverages.

"As to your 'flaw' Dr. Pfister, if anyone from the Czartoryski family can make a watertight case as to their ownership of the Raphael, then my client's adventure is over, and he is out of pocket the option money he paid to me, and any other expenses he may have incurred. I, on the other hand, have secured my non-refundable option payment. Life is a gamble. And life would be dull if we didn't take chances once in a while, don't you agree?"

Bernard Smote replaced the green silk cloth over the painting and gestured for Max to take one of the two chairs nearby. A low teak table on which Max placed his cup and napkin separated the two men.

"So, let's discuss some business. You were good enough to come all this way and I have taken up far too much of your time already."

Max was not about to tell him that this had already been one of the most thrilling afternoons of his life.

Smote finished his milk and pressed his lips to his napkin.

"Do you know which is the longest dog-sled race in the world, Dr. Pfister?"

"Currently it's the Finnmark in northern Norway at 1,200 kilometers. It's not the toughest race in the world. That would be '*The Run*' in Alaska and the Northwest Territories."

"An educated guess, but incorrect."

Max looked at him sharply, puzzled. There was little about the world of racing sled dogs that he did not know. Smote continued.

"No, Dr. Pfister, it's the race that begins in the southern end of the Kamchatka peninsula in Russia and runs northeast to the town of Chukotka. It's 2,100 kilometers in length and is run over 35 days."

"I know that race. It was called the Beringia and was discontinued in 1993."

"On that you are correct. But I have recently been informed that it will be revived this year and set up to be the ultimate test of man and dog. The Russians want to make a statement to the world. Dog-sled racing in Russia is big business with prize money exceeding that of the Iditarod in Alaska. But do you know what makes it most interesting?"

Max was becoming distinctly impatient. His body language must have given him away because his host forced a pause in the conversation.

"Wagering, Dr. Pfister. Wagering. Wealthy Russians like to gamble. A great deal. Wealthy Russians run most of the national companies – telecommunications, smelting, transport, gas and pipelines and the like. And these men – yes, all men, of course – will not only become corporate sponsors of various teams but will place massive wagers on the outcome of the Beringia at its new Guinness Book of World Records length. Needless to say, each man will take every advantage to protect his wager."

"This is all very interesting, sir, but what does it have to do with me?"

"Yes, quite. I am rambling, but I felt that you needed to have some context. You see, I know that you're an expert in the field of breeding and caring for sled dogs, as I mentioned. In fact, I have read your PhD paper on 'Super Dog – Genetic Planning to the Perfect Canine.' It is rather arcane and not an easy read, but I managed to get the gist of it."

Max was again impressed, and even more unnerved.

"So, you want me to purchase sled dogs for you? Is that what this is all about? Because if it is, you've made a mistake."

"Not sled dogs, Dr. Pfister. One specific dog. You are, of course, acquainted with the dog named Ulysses. You probably also know that the sled led by Ulysses defeated all other sleds for the past two years in a row competing in '*The Run*.' An unheard-of feat. And many of the runners-up were using dogs you had bred."

Smote paused for effect, with the phrase 'runners-up' hanging there like icicles – pointed and deadly.

"No, Dr. Pfister, I want you to acquire *a dog*. I want you to acquire *this dog* Ulysses for me. I have a buyer waiting in Moscow."

"I am afraid that's impossible. You know as well as I, sir, that McCord will not sell. He claims some sort of spiritual connection between the dog and his family. Rubbish as far as I'm concerned."

"You will recall in our earlier conversation, we discussed how certain successful entrepreneurs used their imagination to overcome… certain obstacles to obtaining their objectives in the art world? I feel certain that an imaginative and resourceful person such as yourself could find a solution to the problem you faced with this recalcitrant owner."

Max studied this odd little man, trying to be sure he was understanding the message he was sending.

"To be very clear, Dr. Pfister, I want this dog, and I am prepared to make it very much worth your while. Your earlier failures notwithstanding, you are both well qualified and well positioned to accomplish the task I am proposing."

He looked at Max for a reaction. Max willed himself to give none.

"If you accept this contract, I will pay you $250,000."

Max kept his gaze steady — and swallowed hard.

"You will leave here today with $100,000 in cash as an advance to cover any expenses you might incur, and I will send you a bank transfer for a second $100,000 when I see you have the animal in your possession. You will be paid the final $50,000 in cash upon delivery of the dog to me. What do you think? Are you the man for this contract? Or was I wrong in assuming an assignment like this would prove appealing to you? I rather thought it might, given the circumstances around your plane crash, the loss of your pilot's license and your business, medical costs, things like that. And Ulysses's owner's dogs are faring very well on the circuit…"

Max was in a turmoil and he knew he mustn't let it show. He was angry that this man knew so much about him and how deeply his life had been turned upside down by the crash. How his life had been put on a completely different trajectory by a deadhead frozen in a northern lake. How he had struggled to acquire this magnificent once-in-a-lifetime dog and had failed. Twice. Was this all for real? Was this man dressed in white actually going to give him $100,000 in cash and let him walk out the door? He was suspicious because it seemed too easy. But, most of all, he was worried because Max knew that if he accepted this man's money and the contract, his life would start on a completely different trajectory, because there was only one way he could acquire Ulysses. It would be risky, it would be dangerous, and it would be illegal. He shifted in his chair and stared at his empty teacup and the mysterious pattern the leaves made on the bottom. Perhaps they were telling him his fortune. If only he could read them.

"I would be less than honest if I didn't say that this is a very tempting offer. I wouldn't even consider it if I didn't think there was a good possibility that I would be successful in obtaining this animal for you. As it turns out, there may be an opportunity in about six weeks to make that happen."

"The next starting of 'The Run.'"

Once again Max was taken aback by the man's knowledge.

"One detail we need to clarify, sir. What happens if I am unsuccessful in obtaining this dog for you? After all, you will have paid me $100,000 up front."

"I will expect you to return the money."

Max was silent and beginning to feel apprehensive. Smote continued.

"There is little more for us to discuss, Dr. Pfister, and I need your decision. I do not make a habit of giving someone I have never met $100,000, if that's what you are thinking about – and I know you are. All I can add is that I have the ways and the means to safeguard my position."

The not-so-finely veiled threat hung in the air like a socially unacceptable adjective at an elegant dinner party. Max knew that the next words to come out of his mouth would determine the course of his life. He took a deep breath.

"I accept your offer. I will get you your dog."

"I believe you will. You have forty-five days. One final detail. I will communicate with you solely by text, and you with me. This is the secure number."

With that Bernard Smote stood and took a few paces away from the chair, his white-gloved hands clasped behind his back. Max rose also, and once again his gaze fell upon the tall Chinese porcelain jar on the

Lucite stand. He bent over to examine it more closely, first from one side then the other.

"This is an interesting piece."

"Yes, thank you. I like it too. It's Ming."

Max didn't actually say he liked it. But he was curious about it. There was something not quite right about it, but he couldn't put his finger on it.

"May I touch it?" he asked.

The man nodded without comment. Max retrieved the cotton napkin from the coffee table and folded it over the lip at the top. Kneeling down and gripping the jar firmly, he tipped it to about forty-five degrees, and peered at the foot rim on the bottom.

"What are you doing?" There was alarm in the man's voice.

Concentrating on the chore at hand, Max took a white handkerchief from his pocket with his other hand and moistened the corner with saliva. Then he rubbed the moistened cloth around the exposed foot rim, back and forth in a semi-circle.

"Be careful with that! What are you doing? Stop!"

Max stood and carefully returned the jar to its upright position.

"Do you mind my asking where you acquired this piece?"

"None of your business. Now if you…"

"I'm sure you have a provenance for it. Or a Certificate of Authenticity from The British Museum? Something like that?"

"That's not your concern. Why do you ask? You are really being very rude!"

"I am not a professional in this field, but I think I can tell you that this is not Ming. The cobalt blue paint is not Mohammedan Blue. It's too pale. At first, I thought the vase might be the later Qing Dynasty, the period when these objects were made by teams of men as opposed to a single artisan, as was the case during the Ming. But I am afraid that is not the case either."

Smote was becoming quite agitated and a thin bead of perspiration formed on his upper lip. Max watched him impassively and, he had to admit, with some pleasure.

"This jar was probably made in the 1930s or 1940s."

"What on earth are you talking about. That vase is priceless!"

Max unfolded his handkerchief and held it for the man to see.

"Sir, what do you see on my handkerchief?"

Bernard Smote was getting red in the face.

"Why nothing. It's clean."

"Exactly. It is clean. If you look at the foot rim on this jar you will see traces of light brown. Perfectly normal for an object like this to pick up some dust and dirt over the years. But if it was decades-old, the dust and dirt on it would rub off. And it didn't. Why? Because someone applied a varnish-based wash to the foot rim to make it appear like old dirt. That was a very popular device used in the first half of this century to help disguise fakes and counterfeits. I'm sorry to have to tell you this. As I said, I am not a professional and it's possible I am wrong. I don't think so, but it is possible."

Smote's face had gone very red, closer to maroon. He shouted.

"HISA! The package! Then call the car. Dr. Pfister is leaving!"

He turned to look at the porcelain jar as if he had never looked at it before. Hisa reappeared, carrying a small package wrapped in brown silk and tied with ribbon. He approached Max, bowed slightly, eyes to the floor and holding it in two hands, offered it. Then he gestured for Max to follow him. Max turned toward his host, who was bent over the and blue-and-white vase, studying it, rubbing his gloved fingers around the foot rim and staring at them. Max concluded that farewell greetings were not in order, so he turned and followed Hisa to the staircase down to the garage. As he entered the garage, Max heard two sounds. First was the quiet whirr of the starter motor of the limousine, and the second was a muffled scream from upstairs and the sound of cheap Chinese porcelain shattering. Whether Smote knew it was a fake and had been called out as a fraud, or had lost a fortune believing it was authentic, wasn't Max's concern. What did trouble him was that he had turned an adversary into an enemy. On the bright side, he still had a deal with the man, and was about to make a great deal of money. And the way he planned things, what could go wrong?

In the back of the limousine, Max reflected further on his meeting with Bernard Smote. In some ways he envied him — sophisticated, well-connected and probably very rich. But there was a sterility, a lifelessness to the place he had just left. It was devoid of anything personal, anything that told of the owner's taste or personal style. No bric-a-brac, no objects collected from a vacation filled with memories. No, Max concluded, this was a very lonely man. A very angry one and a very dangerous one. He also thought of the momentous decision he had made and the responsibility it entailed. He had agreed to commit a crime, plain and simple. But a quarter of a million dollars was not to be taken lightly. He could pay off the bank loans he had taken to settle his medical bills and get a new truck. Besides, he reasoned, it was all Dan McCord's fault. If he had agreed to sell the dog, none of this would be happening. And he had given the man two chances, after all, and would have paid a fair price. No, Dan McCord was definitely the architect of his own fate. Max stared out the darkened window as the countryside on I-80 North sped by hypnotically. Max's mood took a turn to the dark side, and memories of that dreadful day five years ago came flooding back to him — the day his life changed forever. And today his life had changed forever again. The same sense of foreboding he felt on that day, he was feeling again, right now.

CHAPTER 9

THE CRASH

FIVE YEARS EARLIER

SPRING CAME EARLY TO SOUTHERN ALASKA IN 2011. SOME SAID IT was climate change. It was late May in Juneau and the ice in the harbor was breaking up. Max had a strange sense of foreboding as he revved the engine to check the magnetos on the Cessna 172. The engine sounded good, and the readings on the instruments should have changed his dark mood, but they didn't. He was on the final leg of a charter that began at 7:00 this morning by flying Alice Munroe, a nurse practitioner, to the Native community at Granite Lake.

In the middle of the night he had received an emergency call from the Juneau tower telling him that a woman at Granite Lake about to give birth, was in real difficulty and needed medical care. Alice had volunteered, and the Juneau Medical Officer wanted to charter Good Grace Airlines to fly her up. Max agreed to take off at first light. The flight worked well for him, because he had a stud dog at Granite Lake that was ready to be taken to Twin Forks for another breeding. He wasn't planning to pick up Thorne for two more days but if the dog hadn't done his duty by now, the bitch would be out of estrus.

Although the spring weather had a reputation for being changeable, there was nothing in the meteorological reports to cause concern other than the possibility of localized snow squalls, which he could fly around. An hour after takeoff, the aluminum skis of Max's plane touched down on the packed snow of Granite Lake and he taxied to the dock that serviced the fishing boats in the summer. Two elders and a midwife ran through the stinging, swirling snow as he throttled up to swing his airplane parallel to the dock.

As he was killing the engine, the passenger door opened and Alice Munroe jumped out with her bulging backpack over one shoulder. There was no time to waste, not even on a greeting. All Max could hear were the words 'breech birth' as they hurried along the dock toward the few buildings that made up the community. Perhaps this was the cause of his sense of foreboding. He shut down his airplane and filled in the logbook. He was under no obligation to stay but the situation sounded serious, so he decided to wait a while, just in case a Medivac was called for. He could charge extra for that.

If Granite Lake was famous for anything it was for the sled-dog team put together by Benjamin Lightfoot. For the past four years he had placed in the top five finishers of *The Run*, taking home just enough prize money to breed one of his bitches to a Max Pfister male. So, a week ago Max had flown in with Thorne, picked up a check from Benjamin, and returned to Juneau. He was always careful who he left his stud dogs with but Benjamin, he knew, was honest and had a high respect for dogs, especially Max's. That muted the need for conversation, which suited both men just fine.

Max decided to walk into town and found Benjamin's house. Its occupant was surprised to see Max on his doorstep and invited him in. Reluctantly, Max accepted but declined the offer of tea.

"I've come to pick up Thorne. Did they tie?"

"Yup, I think so," said the other man. "Seeing as how I spent all that money. I was going to help things along if they weren't managing on their own!"

Max's voice took on an edge.

"My dogs always breed. If your bitch wasn't ready, it's no fault of me or my dog. Max Pfister dogs always breed. Now, where is he?"

Benjamin Lightfoot's respect for Max didn't extend to liking him much or at all. Benjamin always bred at his own place, and when he used a Pfister stud, the results were often spectacular.

"I'll get him. They're downstairs."

"In the basement?!" thundered Max. "Get my dog the hell out of there NOW!"

"It's the warmest room in the house Max. And they could have privacy, you know what I mean? I figured they'd like it there. I didn't hear any complaints."

"Get me my dog."

Max took Thorne over to the General Store and bought him a treat, some pemmican, and a pack of Juicy Fruit for himself. He decided to go back to the plane and wait an hour to see if the birthing mother was OK or whether he would have to fly her to Juneau. Plugging the plane's heater into the dock's auxiliary power made it comfortable in a few minutes for man and dog. As the dog curled up on the floor behind him, Max slid a CD in the player and soon the sound of a "Lagrime di San Pietro," written in 1565, filled the cockpit with its acapella beauty. It was only 10:00 o'clock in the morning but the sky was darkening as a small snow squall passed overhead, dropping large, fat snowflakes on the town and its visitors.

"Stay, Thorne," Max commanded and left the plane to walk back to town. He found the clinic and a relieved Alice taking off her bloodied blue latex gloves and throwing them into the garbage.

"The baby's been born, and everything seems okay. She was a partial breech. I was able to turn her just enough." Max looked over at a clearly exhausted mother. A man was kneeling beside the metal bed. The newborn was lost beneath a heap of blankets, a tiny squeak being the evidence of her recent arrival on the planet.

"I'm going to stay overnight because Jennifer and her baby have been through a pretty rough time."

Max nodded as the nurse went about cleaning up her instruments and color-coded bottles.

"If you don't mind flying home alone Max, I can hitch a ride with Sandy White. She's coming in tomorrow with the mail and general store supplies. If I need anything I can radio out."

Max opened the door.

"Suit yourself. And I'm not traveling alone. I've got my dog."

The squall had gone through as quickly as it had come but left a thick dusting of heavy snow on the aircraft.

"I'd better broom her down," Max said to the dog. "Why don't you put that tail to good use and sweep something?"

Twenty minutes later he started the engine and went through his pre-flight check. Fuel ¾ of a tank, oil pressure 70 psi, manifold pressure 32.5, coolant temperature 45 degrees C.

The dark feeling he experienced earlier in the day had returned and Max had no way of explaining it. He was not given to moods though his taciturnity was often mistaken for moodiness. He snapped his seatbelt into place and adjusted the shoulder straps. The six-foot strip of red muslin on top of a 20-foot pole set in the ice gave him the wind direction. He eased the throttle forward and slowly slid away from the dock and into the wind for maximum lift.

He pushed the throttle full forward and with a roar that prompted the dog to look up for a moment, the airplane was airborne. A corkscrew wisp of snow trailed behind each ski for a few seconds as the earth receded below. Max made the decision to fly at 3,000 feet, a little lower than usual. There he could keep an eye on the snow squalls. The last thing any pilot wanted was to find himself on top of a snowstorm with no sight of the ground.

Very quickly, the visibility dropped to about a mile and the ceiling became lower by the minute, requiring Max to descended to 2,000 feet. He could still fly by Visual Flight Rules and the ground, though snowy, was visible. Then the snow started. Max had no sense of where it came from unless he had flown under a storm cloud. Visibility dropped even more, and the wipers struggled to keep the windshield clear of the heavy wet snow. Max looked to the leading edge of his left wing. There was a significant buildup of snow and ice. He would soon be too heavy to remain airborne. He had to land now or crash. The shore of a frozen lake appeared beneath the struggling airplane and Max descended further. The fates had given him a place to land and he had to take advantage of it. There was no time or altitude to do a flyover to check the landing site. He had one shot at it. Slowly he descended, straining through the windshield to find the far shore of the lake; but there was nothing but white, flat featureless white. He set 20 degrees of flap as the icy lake rose to meet him. Thirty feet, 20, 10; the altimeter was useless at this height, and with no horizon, it was impossible to make out the surface of the snow.

THWUMP! The skis hit hard, and Max jerked the throttle back. The aircraft began to slow but what he couldn't see was the 24-inch diameter cedar deadhead protruding from the ice. At 80 miles an hour the right ski hit it straight on, snapping it away from the plane. The right wing dropped and the force of it hitting the ice tore it off. The engine cut out as the prop ground into the snow and ice. Instantly, the aircraft fell further to the right until the stub of the wing root hit the snowy ice, acting like a brake. The airplane cartwheeled end over end over end. It came to rest upside down in a cloud of snow and ice 50 feet from the shore. The only thing the curious wildlife could hear was the distant sound of a 16th century acapella hymn which, after a few seconds, stopped. The silence that was there five minutes ago returned and wilderness became wilderness once more. Silent. Cold. Indifferent.

Max was awakened by a sandpaper tongue licking the blood off his face. Thorne was trying to rouse his master. But Thorne was upside down. Or was it he who was upside down? Pain assailed the wounded man like none other he had ever experienced. The dull pain in his brain was profound and the sharp pain by his right eye unbearable. And, yes, he was upside down, hanging by his seat belt. He tried to unbuckle it with his right hand, but it wouldn't work properly. He didn't need the four years he'd spent in medical school to know his arm was broken. He slowly moved his left hand toward the buckle release. He found it and paused, knowing that he was about to fall down to the roof of the aircraft onto his broken right arm. But he had no choice. He lifted the lever and fell, unaware that he had screamed.

The next thing that seeped into Max's consciousness was the sound of Thorne whining softly with his head resting on his master's chest. He had no idea how long he had been unconscious the second time but judging by the blood that had dried on his face and cracked as he grimaced, it must have been an hour at least. It was not particularly cold as spring was only a few weeks away and the ice in some of the smaller lakes was already beginning to break up. But there was a chilling wind from the northwest at about 20 knots. Slowly Max's head cleared, and he took stock of the situation. His first thought was that both he and the dog were lucky to be alive. Max saw the dog's fur matted with blood and assumed he had been injured. But he soon realized that it was his own blood and, miraculously, the dog appeared unhurt.

The pain in his head subsided slightly but the pain by his right eye was terrible. Instinctively he put his hand to his eye and to his horror felt something hard and sharp protruding from the socket. He concluded it could only be a shard of Plexiglas from the shattered windscreen. As he touched it as gently as he could, streaks of white lightning flashing in his brain and the pain was all but unbearable. He knew he couldn't do anything about his survival as long as the shard was in place. So, by touch alone with the thumb and forefinger of his left hand, he found the protruding end of the splinter sticking out of his right eye. With his heart pounding and a sick feeling in his stomach, he prepared himself. One, two…THREE. To his surprise, there was no pain, just another lightning bolt. But the blood began again, and again Thorne tried to help. Max located the first-aid kit, which hadn't fallen out of the pocket in the door. He tore open a gauze packet, holding the soft cotton pad to his bleeding eye. He gingerly cleaned off the blood around the wound, but his vision remained dark. Perhaps it was the blood preventing him seeing. He pressed the gauze gently against his eye and the drying blood held it in place.

It would be dark in two hours and Max knew he had to get to shore if he had any chance at all of survival. He searched the rear cabin and found his survival pack. Now to get out of the plane and onto the shore. Sitting on the roof and bracing himself against the inverted back of his seat, he pushed at the bent right-side door with all his might. Nothing. It wouldn't budge. He tried again with the same result.

So, he slid along the roof of the cabin and into the cargo area where he took aim at the rear door with both feet. Feet together, he kicked hard, again and again and finally it creaked open and he and Thorne could get out of the wrecked airplane and onto the ice-covered lake.

Together they walked unsteadily toward the shore. Max, in shock, was shaking badly as he searched the shoreline for a place to make some sort of camp. Thorne had run ahead and was already exploring the snowy woods. Twenty feet from the shore Max stopped in his tracks. He heard the unmistakable sound of ice cracking and watched in fear as a small fissure appeared at his feet. Could he run for it? He was only 20 feet away from land. So close. But he couldn't risk falling into the frigid water. It would mean certain death. Then he did what the polar bears do and got down on all fours, spreading his weight over a wider area. Without the use of his right arm, this proved only partially successful. A second deep, throaty crack sounded. Thorne heard the sound and began to walk out onto the ice.

"Thorne, stop!" Max commanded.

The dog obeyed, his eyes riveted on his struggling master. Max flattened his body to the ice so that he was virtually slithering toward the shore. Slowly, yard by yard and foot by foot, he made it to land. He no longer felt pain because the cold was taking control of his body, but he knew he would have to find shelter and make a fire. He stumbled into the woods. Ten feet ahead he saw a shelter under the roots of a fallen tree. This natural pocket would at least provide relief from the wind and allow him to keep a fire going. Matches. Where were his matches? In his survival kit. Had he taken it from the plane? Yes. But where was it? He looked at the ground all around him then back out to the ice.

There it was, right where he had dropped onto the ice so it wouldn't break beneath his feet. Thorne was down by the shore. He saw it too.

"Thorne!"

The dog looked over its shoulder at his master.

"Fetch, Thorne, fetch! Fetch!"

The dog looked out at the ice then back to his master and to the ice once again. Slowly, carefully, he stepped onto the ice and made his way toward the bag. At a hundred and ten pounds he was lighter than Max, but the ice was fragile and sensitive to any weight on it. He reached the bag and, taking one of the handles firmly in his jaws, began to drag it toward the shore. Then, ten feet from the shore, another cracking sound. Another fissure opened directly in front of the dog and he slid into the freezing water.

"Come, Thorne. Come! Come on, Boy!"

The man watched helplessly as the dog struggled to make it to the shore dragging the half floating bag beside him.

As dusk began to surround them, man and dog warmed themselves around a small but adequate fire. Though he wasn't hungry Max knew he must eat so he found some biscuits and dried fruit in the survival kit, which was now crystallizing with ice as the evening temperatures dropped. He was tiring, and the full impact of the events of the day began to affect his body and, as he was beginning to sense, his mind. He knew he wouldn't be able to function much longer. Barely able move because of the fatigue and his injuries, he pulled the waterproof survival blanket around him and put another thick branch on the fire. Placing his head on Thorne's side, he was asleep almost immediately as the big dog's rib cage rose and fell in quiet, peaceful rhythm.

Max wasn't sure whether it was the sound that awoke him or the tensing of Thorne's body. The voices were far away, like down a long corridor; distant yet present at the same time. His hazy brain, forcing itself into wakefulness, counted three, maybe four. They were unmistakable for no other sound in the North is like it. It was the sound of a wolf. The pack had probably smelled the fire and the blood and was drawing closer. Thorne made a guttural growl, deep but quiet. Slowly the dog rose to his feet and stood in front of the fire searching the woods for sight, sound or smell of the intruders. He scented this way and that. For the first time in his adult life, Max was utterly helpless. His rifle was somewhere in the wreckage; all he had was his bush knife. Not much good against a pack of wolves. Thorne growled again, a warning growl this time against the still-unseen wolves. Max willed his brain to think. *Think, man, think. There has to be something…* He went through the checklist he had followed those many months ago when he packed the survival kit. *Blanket, bandages, alcohol, matches, candle, water, alcohol. Aspirin, Very pistol and flares! Yes! The Very pistol That will do it. It was only a flare gun but a direct hit would kill, a near miss will would frighten them off.*

His hands searched the frozen bag and he found what he was looking for – the pistol and 2 flares. *Only two? Where the hell are the other two?* Not much, but something. *Shit!*

The howling now came from the woods behind them and was getting louder. Thorne was able to scent the wolves, which meant they were able to scent him too. The hair around his thick neck bristled in an involuntary reflex to the danger he knew he was about to face. He positioned himself between his master and the circling predators. All Max could do was load the pistol with his good hand and wait. He was tired through to his bones and even the adrenalin that his fight-or-flight reflex was pumping into his bloodstream didn't seem to help.

Then he saw them, barely visible in the darkness that had suddenly fallen. Two wolves were circling from the left and two from the right, one staying slightly back. They were slowly moving closer, sizing up their prey. Occasionally, their eyes would reflect white dots of light from the fire, giving them an otherworldly look. But they were very much of this world, a world of hunger and opportunity and survival. They were no more than ten feet away when Max raised the Very pistol. It suddenly felt like it weighed 50 pounds and, unable to support the weight, his arm dropped down to his lap. *Gotta do it. Gotta do it. Gotta do it.* He willed his arm to take aim and his finger to squeeze the trigger. BANG! The red flare sizzled above the head of the lead wolf and skittered uselessly out onto the ice. But in that moment of artificial light, he saw the two missing flares dropped from the bag, in a straight line from the shore to the shelter.

Emboldened, the lead wolf lunged at Thorne, reaching not for his throat but for one of his forelegs. His fangs clenched on the dog's shin but failed to hold. Thorne howled in pain and struck back lightning-quick, shearing the skin off the wolf's nose. The sight and smell of Thorne's blood quickened the tempo of the wolves's attack. A second wolf lunged at the dog's foreleg and this time got a vice-like grip on it; Max heard the sound of Thorne's leg bone snapping. The dog howled an uncanny howl, which the other wolves took as a sign to redouble their attack. One wolf jumped on his back while the one with the bloodied nose lunged at his throat. The wolf with Thorne's bloody leg clamped in his mouth was dragging the dog into the woods while the other two gripped his flesh beneath thick fur. This dreadful scene played out before Max like some obscene horror film. The fourth wolf, the alpha male, was eyeing his prey, and Max knew that the prey was him. *Focus. Focus. Reload. Which wolf should he shoot?* Could he save Thorne? Should he save himself? *Focus. Steady. Aim.* The big alpha was no more than eight feet away when he lunged. Max squeezed the trigger for the second time. The flare caught the wolf full in the mouth and tumbled him, almost headless, back onto the ice and out of view.

The last glimpse Max had of Thorne was the big dog being dragged into the darkness of the forest, motionless and close to death from loss of blood. A mournful bark stuck in his throat, held there by the vice-like grip of his attacker. It was the last sound the beautiful dog would ever make. Out of sight behind him, Max could hear the growling, slathering noise of the wolves as they tore at the warm flesh of their prey.

The sounds of the wolves feeding on his favorite dog seemed to go on forever. Of all the dogs in his life, Thorne was the only one Max would allow himself to have an emotional bond with. Max buried his face in his hand and let out a cry that began and ended in the darkest corner of his soul.

With their bellies full, and with no alpha to lead them, the three remaining wolves melted into the woods to return to their lair. Sated.

The unearthly silence of the land returned. The fire flickered weakly. And Max fell unconscious.

CHAPTER 10

THE AFTERMATH

MAX FELT WARM. BLESSED, ALL-ENVELOPING WARMTH. IF THIS WAS what it was like to be dead, then it wasn't bad at all. The next sensation was the smell of something he remembered from his youth. It was the smell of bandages. He looked up at the dotted ceiling tiles and the equipment near his bed. Everything looked strange, two-dimensional. Something was wrong. Then he realized that his head was wrapped in bandages and his right eye was covered. He raised his left hand to feel the bandages. As he stirred, his sister Rose stood up from the chair where she had been keeping vigil for the past six hours. She slipped her hand into his and squeezed gently. Thanks to the morphine in his IV drip, Max was feeling no pain, at least not in his body. As his head cleared, when was it, last night, the night before? Images came back to him. And he began to weep softly.

"Rest, my darling, rest."

Rose bent down and kissed the cheek not covered by bandages. All Max could remember was his wonderful dog Thorne being dragged into the woods to be devoured by the wolves. The only one of his dogs he had ever allowed himself to have an inkling of affection for.

"I should have…"

He whispered more to himself than anyone.

"Maybe if I…"

A moment, a minute or an hour later, he didn't know which, Rose was gone, and the door opened. A forty-something man in a red-checked lumberjack shirt with a stethoscope around his neck walked over to him.

"Hey Mr. Pfister, you're one lucky son-of-a-bitch. Two more hours on the ground and hypothermia woulda got you. Or maybe the wolves would have come back."

"The wolves…"

Max paused, straining to remember.

"How'd I get… here?"

"You're actually a double lucky guy, Mr. Pfister. Turns out that this morning, Sally White was on the same vector to Juneau as you were flying, and she saw the wreckage of your plane. Naturally, she landed and here's where you become a triple lucky son-of-a-bitch. She had nurse Munroe on board. They had to sidestep a wolf out on the ice with most of its head blown off, and they found you dead to the world. At first, they thought you were actually dead, but no, you were still in the land of the living – barely. They dragged you to the plane, managed to get you in the cargo space, and here you are. Sally radioed ahead so we were ready for you, and on the way down, nurse Munroe cleaned you up pretty well and stabilized your arm."

Max was silent, trying to understand everything. The doctor sat on the end on the bed. There was more to come.

"I am very sorry, but we couldn't save the eye. The optic nerve had been cut and because there was some muscle damage as well, there was no choice but to remove it."

"Aw, shit…" was all Max could say as he tried to process this information.

"They're doing great things with prosthetics these days. Believe it or not, they're making them out of coral, so there are no rejection issues, and the remaining eye muscles have something to attach to and..."

"I don't want a glass eye! No way. I don't want to know about it."

The doctor stood and was quiet for a moment.

"I've set your right wrist. You will be able to start physio in about six weeks. It should heal to be like new."

Max lifted his arm off the bed and looked at the heavy white plaster.

"The only other injury I could find was a badly bruised sternum, not broken but it took quite a hit. Probably when you were thrown against the steering column. To come through a crash like that at all makes you one lucky son-of-a-bitch. I'll look in on you tomorrow morning."

Max was left alone to try to make some sense of what was to become of his family, his work, his life.

And he didn't feel good about any of it.

Max was stirred from the morphine-induced sleep by the sound of a woman's voice. Distant, hollow, fuzzy.

"Wha...? Who...?"

"Shhhh, Max. You have to rest. I came up as soon as I heard. I am your sister after all, right? The doctor said we could come back for short visit. Bobby's here too."

Rose gestured to her son, who was standing in the corner barely able to look up.

"Come and say hello to your uncle, Bobby."

Slowly, the 12-year-old boy walked to the side of the bed and looked down at the broken figure of his once-perfect father-figure.

"You're blind you know!" he shouted. "They took out your fucking eye and fucking threw it away! And the insurance company says you screwed up. They won't pay for your plane. You're pathetic!"

He sobbed and turned and ran out the door into the hall. Max lay motionless. Bobby's rant was nothing compared to what Max's father had managed on a slow day.

"Is that true about the insurance?"

"Max, we'll talk again tomorrow. I've got to see to Bobby."

"Rose, is it true?"

His voice was hard and demanding.

"I've got to go to Bobby. I'll ask the doctor to come in. I love you Max. Everything will be all right, you'll see."

And she kissed him again. He turned his head away from her and heard the sound of the door clicking closed.

Max fell into a terrible depression. He refused to accept any help for his condition or even acknowledge that it existed. He became sullen, withdrawn and even more taciturn. In his view he was a man on whom the fates had played a cruel trick. The loss of his eye was, well, an inconvenience. He could see perfectly well with the remaining one. No, that wasn't the problem. The problem was that he would never fly an airplane again. Invisible men in glass towers in Juneau had declared it an "at fault" accident. "Pilot error," they said. There was even the possibility they wouldn't cover his medical bills. And if that wasn't enough, he heard that the Department of the Environment was thinking about making him pay for the cleanup and disposal of his wrecked aircraft. "Environmental Protection" the bureaucrats called it. As it turned out, the spring melt took care of the problem. But there is no place in the skies for a one-eyed pilot. Never again would he feel the exhilaration of a Lycoming engine at the moment he pushed the throttle full in on takeoff. No more winter sunsets from 5,000 feet that nourished the spirit and cleansed the soul. And perhaps most difficult of all, no more solitude. Gone were the hours when at cruising altitude a man can be totally alone with his thoughts, and the mind was free to travel into every nook and dark corner of its existence. And in that place, it can dream and scheme, find peace and turmoil, and think thoughts too dark to ever be formed into words. Those were the moments when he imagined retribution on the board members who had suspended his medical license. Or the patient infliction of pain he wished he'd visited upon his father, and likely would have, if the stupid, drunk bastard hadn't wrapped his 65 Chevy Impala around a Douglas Fir that wouldn't bend.

The white Mercedes deposited Max where he had been picked up. Exactly where he had been picked up, then sped away silently. Max returned to his office. He had some thinking to do and some very serious plans to make. Life-changing plans.

CHAPTER 11

ULYSSES BEGINS HIS JOURNEY

PRESENT DAY

ULYSSES STAYED CONCEALED IN THE BUSHES UNTIL HE SAW THE MAN leave his truck and go into the building. The low rough bushes he was hiding in were sparse and he knew he would soon have to be out in the open. He had never seen land like this where dust made his eyes sting and filled his nose. He saw large birds floating high above, flying without flying, circling effortlessly and endlessly. Try as he might, he could scent no wildlife though he did see in the distance a small brown animal poking its head up from a hole in the ground. To Ulysses, it looked something like a beaver, but it was much smaller and lighter in colour. But it was the sky and the sun that dominated his world. He had seen a perfectly blue sky before in the North, many times. But the sun here was different. It seemed larger and definitely hotter than any sun he had ever felt. He found himself both drawn to it and repelled by it at the same time. It was warm and comforting but also, he sensed, dangerous. And as the sun beat down on him, Ulysses began to sweat through his tongue, and he panted. He knew he would soon be thirsty and would need water. So, staying about 20 feet off the road, Ulysses took the first of a million steps on his journey home. As he would learn in the coming weeks and months, an unseen force, an energy, would orient him north, like the pointer on a compass. The same mysterious forces that for millennia have guided migrating birds and butterflies were guiding Ulysses. He did not have the power to understand it, but he knew it was real, and it was strong, and it would be his guide. His spirit guide. He would follow its inexplicable call.

Two bours later, with the sun magnifying its punishment on the world below, the vegetation changed. The dust was behind him and everything became greener. He passed huge fields, immaculately ordered with row upon row of green plants. An automatic watering device caught his attention as it rhythmically squirted a stream of water far out onto the field. This could be the answer to his thirst. He cautiously approached the apparatus, which was at about his shoulder height. He watched the tick-tick squirt-squirt motion for a moment, could wait no longer, then leaped at it and bit at it – with miserable results. He barely wetted his mouth, and a lot of the water went into his ear. He shook his head, hard. He waited a moment then tried again, with the same disappointing results. What little water did go into his mouth hurt him because the force was strong. Discouraged, unsatisfied and still thirsty, Ulysses resumed his journey. In this vast farmland Ulysses saw very few humans, which suited him just fine. Later he found himself in an almond grove where the shade was welcome, and he decided to rest a while. He scented water nearby, a lot of water, and he sought it out. His path caused him to leave the verdant countryside. The land became dry again and the row upon row of rich crops became a memory. He found himself on the banks of a man-made river. This was part of the California Aqueduct system. He had never seen a river this wide. At least as wide as 25 sled-dog teams, maybe 50! There was a foot path running alongside it on his side, and a single lane roadway over on the other. Half-sliding, he made his way down the gray earth and shale embankment to the water's edge where he drank and drank to his heart's content. Back on his path, with the afternoon air cooling slightly, Ulysses was making progress and feeling good. Suddenly, he stopped in his tracks. There, in the distance on the opposite roadway, was the black pickup of the man with one eye and the hard stick. Though separated by the enormous distance, and with no way for the man to cross it, no bridges, no cross paths, Ulysses was fearful. He stood with his eyes riveted on the truck as it slowly moved down the road to a point directly opposite him. The man in the long black coat and hat had gotten out of the truck and was casually leaning against it, arms folded. The man looked like a black stain on a piece of gray flannel. Even though they were the length of many sled-dog teams apart, Ulysses could see the white bandage on his cheek. The opponents stood motionless, each looking at the other as if waiting for the dance to begin. And there they stood, neither wanting to be the first to move. Who would blink first? Who would show weakness? If thoughts could fly through the air, Ulysses would know of Max's frustration and anger at being so close yet so far. His casual demeanor belied the turmoil within. At the exact moment that Ulysses chose to resume his journey, Max turned to get into is truck. Ulysses turned his back on the man and the footpath and went overland toward a grove of green bushes a half a mile away. Though he knew he was creating a distance between him and the man, he was still fearful. The memory of his terrible journey was still deep and vivid. He had his freedom to be sure, but he knew the man was clever and would never give up his pursuit. But Ulysses knew he was clever, too. It was a different kind of cleverness, based not on maps or GPS or radio signals; his was a cleverness born of generations of survival. He could travel at night, and he would. He could travel in any kind of weather, and he would. And he knew his greatest advantage was that he could go where the roads could not. And he would do that too. Whatever it took to stay away from the man, and to get back to his home, he would do.

The following morning, Ulysses came upon a real river. Not a man-made one like yesterday, but a big river that flowed and babbled and had shores that wound around rocks and trees. There would be food here. Instinctively, he knew he needed to travel in the direction where the river came from, not to where it was going. His spirit guide told him the right way was north. So, Ulysses followed the Sacramento River for its full 700 hundred miles up to the foot of Mount Shasta, whose peaks and shoulders created the snow melt that birthed that grand river ten thousand years ago.

CHAPTER 12

SOLEIL SAVES A CHILD

THE PHONE RANG IN THE CABIN. DAN ANSWERED IT. SOLEIL WAS outside with Akkisuktok hanging up the washing. The late afternoon sun cast a deep orange-yellow hue.

"Hello? Yes. My God! Soleil. Come quick! Here, take the phone. I'll be at the truck."

Akkis dropped the towel back into the hamper, puzzled.

"Honey, look after your mother. I'll be back soon."

Dan jogged down the gravel path toward his truck, which was 10 years old and courageous. Soleil finished the call and followed Dan, Akkis half a pace behind her.

"Dan, I'll call Dr. Tall Pine and he'll have someone waiting outside his place with a bag for me. You won't have to stop. Now GO!"

Dan did a U-turn and the truck was soon on the highway and a hundred yards away. Soleil watched him go, and she was afraid. Akkis reached up and took her hand, her blue eyes searching.

"Daddy said I should take care of you."

"And you're doing a wonderful job, my darling. But I have to get some things ready."

"What happened?

"Well, do you remember how Daddy and I told you about those ponds near the old gold mines? And how you must never go near them?"

Akkis nodded as Soleil pinned the last two articles on the line.

"Well, a boy just a little older than you was playing hockey on one of those ponds and the ice broke and he fell in. He was able to get out and he ran home to his mother who washed him, but he started to vomit and develop a temperature. He may have swallowed some of the bad water. We don't know. We're a lot closer than the clinic in town, so his mother wants to bring him here. She's a Dene woman and believes in the strength of traditional medicine."

"Is he going to die?"

"I don't know. But it's very serious."

"What's in the pond?"

"It's a very, very bad thing darling. It's called arsenic."

Soleil's gift was about to be put to the test as she waited for Dan to return with the stricken boy. Soleil took the almost empty blue plastic hamper into the cabin. She left the door open and Akkis watched her mother prepare a bed for the boy with fresh white sheets. She filled a large pot of water from the well hand-pump beside the sink and turned on the propane stove. Then she pulled down a small wicker basket from a high shelf and examined the contents, selecting some and putting them on a metal baking sheet.

"What's that, Mommy?"

"These are some special barks and plants that will help the boy."

The light changed quickly as the sun fell behind the big pines. The dogs in the pens were the first to hear Dan's truck as it turned off the highway, and they gave him their usual noisy greeting. Dan drove as close to the cabin as he could, lifted the limp seven-year-old from his mother's lap, and carried him inside the cabin. The mother followed but Soleil gently stopped her at the door and took the bag from the pharmacy from her.

"Marie, you will have to leave him here with me. Dan, take Marie and Akkis to your father's house. You can come back in the morning. Until then there's nothing you can do except leave me and the boy alone. The gods and the spirits have work to do and I will help them as best I can."

"Oh, my baby!" wailed the mother.

She brushed by Soleil, fell to her knees and hugged her comatose son, possibly for the last time. As she left, Soleil felt sure she knew the right potion to create for this child. But her mind went back to last summer when the family that fishes Pigeon Lake, 14 miles away, arrived on their doorstep at midnight with their eight-year-old daughter in their arms. The child was febrile, running a temperature of 103 degrees Fahrenheit. Her clothes were wet with sweat and her breathing, shallow. Soleil knew she didn't have the knowledge to help this child, so Dan drove her into the Stanton Territorial Hospital in Yellowknife with its skeleton overnight staff. The on-call doctor came in as quickly as she could, but it was too late. The peritonitis from her burst appendix had taken her life. Soleil had tortured herself ever since with the thought that there must have been something she could have done. These self-doubts haunted her as she began to attend to the poisoned boy.

Dan began the 20-mile drive into Yellowknife. He pulled the headlights on but had no desire to do the same with the radio. Marie was beside him in the front staring vacantly out the side window, and Akkis was in the back having a quiet conversation with her dolly. Going to his father's house always reminded Dan of a very dark time in their relationship, and in his own life. It was three years ago, but every detail of that event was as clear in his memory as if it had happened last week. He shuddered.

CHAPTER 13

THE RACE, THE STORM

THREE YEARS EARLIER

DAN MCCORD AND HIS FATHER HAD THEIR RESPECTIVE TEAMS AND sleds ready for the 2013 start of 'The Run.' The dogs yelped their impatience and gave 'let's get to it' tugs at their harnesses. Two teams, two sleds. Dan with a young and inexperienced two-year-old Ulysses as his lead, and his father with an experienced dog in every harness. His father was furious at Dan for registering without telling him. His scowl bit deeper than the wind.

"You and the dog, you're both racing too young – especially with this storm comin' in. Too dangerous."

He forbade Dan to race and the young man was conflicted. Dan was over 18 and could do what he wanted. He would fight it out with his father after the race. He buried his face in Ulysses's neck and whispered, "We'll show him."

The race started with a ten-minute spacing between each sled. The father, at Number 2, and Dan and Ulysses as the last, the number 12 sled. Soleil and Akkis were in the crowd, warm in sealskin parkas. Like most northern mothers, Soleil had sewn an *amaut* into her parka that allowed the naked two-year old Akkis to snuggle against her mother's bare back in a special sealskin pouch. Baby-wearing at its most primal and efficient, it makes a privileged space for mother and child. At 6:00 o'clock at this time of year in these latitudes, it looks and feels like the middle of the night. Big diesel generators powered the floodlights in the paddock area and at the start line. With all the other teams on their way, Dan's start time came up and he and his team jerked into action. He mushed past the disapproving looks from the organizers. They think his father is right. With a wave and a kiss blown to Soleil and their daughter, Dan was off. The weather continued to worsen. The wind picked up and the temperature went down.

Four hours out and the Arctic countryside was completely obscured. Dan, Ulysses and the team were in the middle of a vicious blizzard. Fifty mph winds with temperature dropping fast – now minus 20 Fahrenheit – '20 below.' Any colder and he would have to stop and wrap each dog's genitals in rabbit fur. It was a whiteout. The snow made the trail and the markers invisible. A seasoned lead dog might be able to find the way, but Ulysses was too young, too inexperienced. They were just plain lost. Dan had to stop and go into survival mode. Fast. He unhitched the dogs from the sled and, fighting the stinging wind, tethered them to a tree. In the light from the xenon headlamp strapped to his head Dan could do nothing as the sled slid slowly away into the night. No time to go after it. Situation critical. The dogs formed a circle and lay down with each other for warmth. Ulysses found a fallen tree trunk and, searching for sight of Dan, barked into the blowing whiteness. Dan followed the sound and together they took cover in its lee. Dan realized this was a life-and-death situation. The weather deteriorated further with the temperature dropping another 10 degrees. Total blizzard. Total whiteout. A disaster in the making. Human and dog hunkered down as best they could. Dan buried his head in Ulysses's soft underbelly and in no time the snow covered them both completely.

The Race, The Storm

His eyes told of his unspoken fear as his headlamp flickered in their snowy cave. He turned it off to save whatever power was left.

Dawn came late in these northern latitudes. When it did, the blizzard had passed, and the sky was blue and clear. A bright sun illuminated the brittle snow-covered countryside but offered no warmth to the lifeless forest. The branches of the pines drooped to the ground struggling for dignity under the massive snow loads. Sharp cracks declared victory for gravity as tree limb after tree limb succumbed to the crippling weight. A hawk landed on the branches of a leafless Maple. His flinty eyes examined the desolate scene before him. Suddenly, movement. His head snapped around – ever alert. Is it danger or is it prey? The snow, which almost obscured a big fallen tree trunk, was moving. The hawk remained completely immobile. Even his feathers were still in the bitter air, and his remarkable vision focused on the movement.

The snow moved again. A snout emerged. The snout of a dog. It pushed out into the air and Ulysses's large white head emerged into the frigid morning. With a little struggle he freed himself from the snow's lethal embrace. He shook himself. Took in his surroundings. Turned back to the snowbank and began digging furiously. All the curious hawk could see was the animal's hind quarters, and snow spraying out from between his legs. The digging stopped as he began to pull at something. A man appeared on his hands and knees. Slowly he stood and he too shook himself, brushing the snow from his parka as his eyes adjusted to the light. With no meal in sight the hawk rose from his perch and wheeled away.

"Hey Ulysses, how'ya doing?"

He scuffed the big dog's ears. Ulysses looked past him to the desolate countryside.

"You're right. This is shit."

The sound of a human voice aroused the other dogs tethered a few yards away and they too broke free of the thick blanket of snow one by one. There was no sign of the sled – or the trail they came on. Dan checked his wrist compass/thermometer. It read 38 below zero. Human skin will freeze in less than five minutes.

The dogs began to yelp and dance.

"All right, we're all hungry," Dan shouted with anger and worry. "But I don't know where the hell the sled is! I don't even know where I am."

He looked to Ulysses conspiratorially.

"Yeah, no food, no body heat."

Ulysses looked up at him steadily. Dan returned his gaze. More words were unnecessary. Hunger began to agitate the dogs, and all but one were yelping their demands. The smallest of the dogs was quite still. Blank brown eyes looked at nothing in particular. Dan unclipped him and carried him to the snow cave that protected them last night. He opened his parka and wrapped it around the dog, pressing the animal to his body. He just managed to zip it closed again.

The afternoon light began to darken. The dogs were still restless from their hunger and, with the sun disappearing, even they felt the searing cold. Dan was huddled in the snow cave; only his eyes were visible through the fur trim of his parka. Ulysses was nowhere to be seen.

"Ulysses!" he shouted. "Here boy! Ulysses!"

A few minutes later Ulysses returned, out of breath and with snow caked to his underbelly.

"Where the heck have you been? I don't suppose you found a McDonald's or something, did you?"

Ulysses looked up at him. Dan checked his wrist thermometer and took a breath.

"It's still nearly 40 below. Gonna be a bitch of a night."

He looked down at the dog, saddened by the fate he had given them both.

"Dad was right." And, as an afterthought, "I hope he's OK."

Something caught Ulysses's attention and he cocked his head and looked into the distance.

'What…!?"

Dan's eyes strained into the white nothingness. Ulysses turned this way then that way, searching. Then he was still.

"This goddamned cold. What?"

A moment later Dan heard it too. The 'thwump thwump thwump' of helicopter blades as they slapped at the thin cold air struggling to stay airborne.

"Oh shit! YES!"

As he stood, the little dog slid out of his parka and onto the snow. Dan hollered and beat his arms and hollered some more. He waved and screamed and jumped up and down and screamed some more. He could even read the words *'Madelena Mining'* on the belly of the chopper as it passed overhead - and continued on its flight path. The pilot had not seen them. Dan stood dumfounded then fell to his knees. A deep cry came up out of his belly, a cry of utter hopelessness. He buried his face in his hands as the pain and realization of his fate came pouring out. Tears froze on his cheeks like tiny pearls, never to fall to the ground. He lay on the white snow, curled into a ball and quietly cursed it for concealing him from the helicopter's crew.

"I just want to sleep…to sleep…"

"Hey bud!"

The man's voice shouted. It sounded to Dan like it was coming through a long sewer pipe.

"Hey buddy, we gotta get outta here. There's not much light left."

Dan's head cleared. Ulysses nose-nudged him in the rump. He stumbled to his feet, helped by a man with a flight suit under his parka.

"Just over that ridge. Only place I could land was on the ice on the pond. Come on. We got no time to waste."

Dan scooped up the little dog under his arm.

The pilot and Dan and Ulysses made their way the 50 yards to the idling chopper. It was a small two-seater Bell 106J with cargo in boxes behind the two seats.

"Come on. Jump in and buckle up. We gotta boogie!"

"But what about my dogs? Ulysses? What about the team?"

"Look, if the weather holds and the company says it's OK, we can come back tomorrow with the Jet Ranger. It'll take 6 people so it can haul 12 dogs. But like I said, that all depends on what the boss says, and the weather."

Dan looked at Ulysses.

"I can't do this. I can't leave them here to starve. To die! They're... they're... my team!"

"Listen, you have exactly 30 seconds to decide what the hell it is you want to do because I have to be out of here before it gets any darker. I have no intention of putting my overnight survival gear to the test. Not in the cards. So, make up your damn mind, kid. RIGHT NOW!"

The pilot turned his attention to the console, grumbling. As he reached out to the waiting switches, he stopped.

"Wait a minute. Maybe this'll work. I was delivering supplies to the drilling rig at Red Lake. They're in the back. Three of those six boxes are food, the rest is fuel and parts and stuff like that. I'll probably catch shit when I get back, but we can dump that food on the dogs. The boxes'll break when the hit. At least they'll have something for the night."

Dan was tortured by his terrible dilemma

"Look, I just used up half of your 30 seconds with my plan. Make up your mind."

Dan looked at Ulysses.

"OK, but Ulysses comes with us."

"Oh, fer chrissake. Let's go. Carry the dog on your lap until we dump the food then he can ride in the back. Deal?"

"Quit talking and fly this thing, will you?"

With the pilot's attention directed toward the dials and controls, Dan slid the little dog behind his seat, and buckled up. He held tight to Ulysses.

They lifted off and hovered over the dogs. The pilot reached across and popped the latch on Dan's door. Holding on to Ulysses on his lap with one hand, Dan reached behind him with the other and shoved three boxes out the door into the swirling snow.

"OK," hollered the pilot. "Latch your door, put the dog behind the seat and we're out of here."

Then, as an afterthought,

"Are you sure you didn't dump the drill bits onto the dogs?"

With little effort, Ulysses climbed over Dan's shoulder into the newly emptied space, company for the small, sad stowaway. The pilot wheeled the helicopter around, found some altitude and headed west into the setting sun. In a few minutes the cabin was warmed by the heat from the engine and Dan took off his heavy parka.

"I thought you'd missed us," he shouted.

The pilot gave him a 'I-can't-hear-you' sign and pointed to a set of headphones and a mic hanging from the top of the cabin. Dan snugged them into place.

"I said, I thought you'd missed us!"

"I did," the pilot replied. "It was totally white down there. A big blank. Then I saw the packed snow."

"Packed snow?"

"Yeah, the snow at the north end of the pond. About 20 feet around."

Dan tried hard to understand what the pilot was saying.

"That was really smart of you to do that 'cause it was obviously man-made. And where the dogs were tethered? I could have flown over you all day and not seen you."

Dan quietly shook his head in disbelief. He reached behind him to feel Ulysses's fur.

He returned the headphones to their hook. His head fell back against the seat and he closed his eyes. His right hand reached back to Ulysses's paw.

""No, it wasn't man-made" he said to no one in particular. "You son-of-a-bitch of a dog. Literally."

It looked bad. Very bad.

Three days of searching with three helicopters and four fixed-wing aircraft had located only five teams. They were the ones who, like Dan, had started late and were behind the leader group. Three of the teams had spent two nights in the minus 40 temperatures. The drivers had been airlifted out suffering dehydration, exposure and frostbite. The other two teams had it worse. They had to suffer through a third night on the ground. They were found beside their sleds, which meant they had some food. Not much, and even less water because the idea was to keep the sled as light as possible and take food and water from the pre-arranged caches along the route.

Much to Dan's relief, the mining company authorized the airlift of his team the next day. He flew in to wrangle them into the aircraft and secure them there. Because they had eaten, they were manageable.

Andrew Darlington had to have two fingers on his left hand amputated along with the big and little toe on his right foot. Part of his nose had been frostbitten and Doctor Newbery was doing his best to keep it on his face. Dave Thompson was unconscious when they found him. And they only found him because his starving team had dug through the new snow right down to muskeg in a desperate effort to find something to eat. The big brown patch was easy to see from the air. No one was sure whether Dave would survive. Doc Newbery gave him no better than a 30 percent chance. And if he did make it, he would be horribly disfigured. To make matters worse, to get him back immediately they had to leave his dogs behind. Three days without food had turned them wild and the pilot reported that he saw at least one partly devoured carcass. His paramedic was able to get close enough to release them from the sled, but not from their harness. Some might survive the wolves and the bear. The strong ones might even make it home.

Maybe.

The real tragedy, however, was with the other six teams. Six drivers and seventy-two dogs were missing. Because even lithium batteries fail at such extreme temperatures, the locator beacons were useless. The search had to be totally visual. Although the route was easily seen on the map, looking at the blank, white ground, even from less than 1,000 feet, the likelihood of finding anybody or anything was extremely small. The fourth day of the search had to be called off when the weather turned. The zero-visibility system and the minus 50 degree temperatures hung over the area for the next week. All hope of finding any survivors was, quite simply, abandoned. In the profoundly bitter cold, Dan's father curled in his sealskins, and huddling with the dogs, struggled to fight off the all-consuming desire to sleep. He wasn't cold anymore; he just needed to sleep.

Eighty miles away, at 5:16 that morning, Ulysses awoke. He circled two or three times then pointed his nose toward the stars and let out a howl. The kind of howl his breed had been sounding for a hundred generations. A keening, grieving sound so intense it could only mean one thing.

At that moment, Dan's father died.

'The Run' had killed again.

That was three years ago but it still made him deeply sad to think about it, though he continued to marvel at Ulysses's mysterious sense of distant loss, an attribute shared by many canines. Dan pulled into the driveway of his father's house. He knew he had to sell it eventually, but he couldn't bring himself to do it. Not yet. Dan knew that his father's fate had nothing to do with his being in the race. He knew he wasn't responsible, but he still felt guilty. And the house was, well, a part of his life. His father had lived there for 40 years, and his father before. Dan and his sister were born in it, and his mother had died in it. It was just too full of friendly ghosts. He would wait a little longer to sell 'The McCord Place.' Or maybe move into it. Akkis' school and all. It wasn't a fancy house, but it was sturdy and warm; built just after the Second World War. Families from across the Dominion of Canada and beyond were coming to Yellowknife for the work. The Giant Mine poured its first gold brick in June of '48. As a child, Dan heard the rumour that the famous 'Johnny' Baker who, with a partner, held the initial 'Giant' claims, had lived here. Dan's grandfather, recently demobilized from the 48th Highlanders after the war, arrived here from Ayrshire, Scotland, with a young bride in tow and some money in his purse. He was the first owner. 'A stout house,' his grandfather would call it.

On the second floor, the door to the room where his mother and father had slept was closed, but the other three bedrooms came in handy. Dan and Soleil had one, and he would stay in it with Akkis tonight. Dan prepared one of the other rooms for Marie. It had been a hard day for them all, especially Marie, who was asleep in minutes. Akkis, in the adjacent room, followed very quickly. Dan went downstairs into the living room and turned on the small reading light beside his father's favorite chair. It was placed 'just so' in relation to the huge stone fireplace. Beside the fireplace was an ancient cabinet that served as a liquor cabinet – among many other uses, but it was that purpose that beckoned to Dan this evening. A splash of his favorite Laphroaig kissed the bottom of the heavy glass in his hand. He settled into the soft leather chair filled with creases and character and memories.

As Dan sat in the half-light, his memory danced with images of all the birthday parties, family get-togethers, Christmas tree dressings and his wedding reception. His eye returned to the ancient cabinet against the wall which, until he was 10, had just enough space behind it for him to hide from his grandfather. That wonderful man, who always enjoyed a game of hide-and-seek, always rewarded Dan with a cuddle on his lap in front of the fire. His grandfather always smelled nice. Tobacco and tweed. 'And a touch of heather," he would say. Dan also remembered the meetings of the Arctic Rangers, or Canadian Rangers as they were properly called. A voluntary unit of the Canadian Armed Forces reserve, its members provided a military presence in sparsely settled areas and remote communities. Dan had been elected as the Sergeant of the 1st Canadian Ranger Patrol Group, based in Yellowknife, a tribute to the esteem in which he was held by Inuit, First Nations, Métis, and other residents in the area. Their main job was search and rescue, usually on the ground as the aircraft searched overhead. They were also called on to fight wildfires or flooding. But what Dan was remembering on this evening was the feeling of camaraderie he and his 12 or 15 fellow Rangers shared as they drank beer, traded stories and were just plain happy in each other's company. The old-fashioned wallpaper, and post-war lighting fixtures his grandmother loved, bore silent witness to the conviviality and friendship that had filled this room over so many years.

More recently, Soleil had used it for what she called 'Health Circles,' where Healers and health practitioners from throughout the community would come together. She was one of only two midwives among the group and always anxious to share her knowledge. Some participants had Healers as parents and grandparents and great-grandparents, and they all wanted to keep the traditional knowledge and ways alive. While they all respected modern medicine and the community healthcare system, there were some things their forebears just did better. Differently and better. It was also a place where, under Soleil's compassionate and intelligent supervision, all cultural groups, including some recent European and Middle Eastern additions, would live and work in harmony. This was also a perfect place for the parents of preschoolers to use while the new daycare was under construction. Dan could almost hear their laughter and playful commotion filling the big, dark, warm room. Being a part of the history of 'The McCord Place' gave Dan a sense of place and heritage that he shared with Soleil and Akkis of course, but also with anyone who was searching for those values, or who had been forced to leave them behind in their country of birth.

Marie, worried about her son, had slept fitfully. She awoke at 5:00 a.m., paced upstairs then downstairs, then upstairs again, finally knocking on Dan's door at 6:00. He understood her need to get back to the cabin. Akkis, rubbing her eyes, was a little less understanding, but very soon they were all in the truck headed to the bakery for a sweet roll, a coffee, a donut, a cup of tea, a bagel, a container of milk or whatever was necessary to start the day and keep them busy on the drive to the cabin. Dan ordered a large cup of hot water into which he put a bag of lapsang souchong, Soleil's favorite tea, which he had found in the kitchen cupboard.

Soleil and the boy were sitting outside the cabin on the big tree stump. He was between her legs like an animated cello; her long, flowered dress picked up pine needles around its hem. Soleil had her arms around the boy not to protect him but to feel the motion and energy of his young body; his life force now returned to normal. As usual, the dogs announced Dan's return well before the truck was in sight. Soleil took the boy's hand and they walked toward the place where Dan would park. They were standing there as the pickup came in, and even before it had stopped Marie was out of the passenger's seat and on her knees hugging her son. She couldn't control her tears of joy.

"Mommy. Why are you crying? Are you sad?"

Marie was speechless, and she picked up her boy and started to laugh and did a dance around the clearing, accompanied by the chorus of dogs barking in the near distance. What beautifully mismatched dancing partners they made! Akkis buried her face in her mother's skirts, gave her legs a big hug and inhaled her fragrance. Her mother always smelled so… so…perfect! Dan put his arm around Soleil's shoulder, and they looked deep into each other's eyes. Soleil gave him an almost imperceptible nod of affirmation, and he broke into a big toothy blue-eyed grin.

"Come," said Soleil. "Let's all have some breakfast."

CHAPTER 14

ULYSSES AND THE GIANT WHIRLPOOL

THE NEXT FULL MOON WAS BARELY VISIBLE THROUGH THE SCUDding clouds. A brisk rain shower at dusk had confined Ulysses to his sheltering place. When the moon was full up in the sky and the rain had moved on, Ulysses arose and left. He found the stream and began to follow it once more. As the clouds cleared it became quite bright and Ulysses recognized many of the landmarks he had seen before. Through the night he made his way along the bank as the river gradually announced its new size and power. And the river developed a voice, a voice like Ulysses had never heard before. It thundered and gurgled and said, *'Trespass carefully.'* As dawn broke, Ulysses rested and watched the morning light reveal the new day, and for him, a new world. The shore on which he had been traveling all night was mounded with massive boulders as if there had been a landslide two years ago or 200 years ago. He looked downstream and saw that the water appeared calmer not far away. On the far shore was a lush green meadow, which would make for much easier going. Ulysses made a decision to make for the calmer water downstream where he could easily swim to the far side. Slowly and carefully he made his way through the rock field. He jumped up onto a rock only to find himself sliding back down with outstretched claws, unable to stop his descent and leaving eight parallel scratch marks. He chose a different path and was able to get past that barrier. He continued to pick his way painstakingly through the rock field until he found himself in what looked like a dead end. He could hear the river not far away and he could scent the fresh water, but he couldn't see it. His eyes searched all the cracks and crannies but to no avail. It looked like he could go no further and would have to double back. But his nose picked up a strong scent of water spray just around a corner up ahead, so he went to investigate. There was a natural arch formed by two resting rocks through which he could see the river beyond. The hole was not big but perhaps just big enough for him to squeeze through. Ulysses sat and looked at it as the water beyond beckoned. He approached the arch and poked his head and shoulders through. It was very tight, but he managed to wiggle and pull until his head and shoulders and front paws were on the river side. He felt the rocks gripping his ribs tightly. His forepaws were out in front of him while his hind paws remained on the land side. And there he stayed. His hind legs had no purchase and were pushing uselessly into the air. His forepaws, though they could almost touch the water, also had nothing to grip. Ulysses was good and stuck. He twisted this way and back but nothing. He was unable to budge forward or back. He was panting hard through both exertion and stress, and he knew he needed to calm down. When a young forest fox went to the river pool to drink, he beheld a strange sight. There above him, protruding from the rocks was what looked like half a white wolf. Its back legs were moving but it was going nowhere. The fox could not see his head and his jaws, so he knew it wasn't dangerous His instinct told him to check this creature more closely. The fox approached slowly, and avoiding the sometimes-flailing legs, which could break his back, managed to get his nose close to Ulysses's anus and genitals. On the other side of the rock, Ulysses froze, ears back, eyes wild. Something was sniffing him, and very thoroughly. With no sense of what it was, from a chipmunk to a Grizzly bear, Ulysses panicked, and with every ounce of strength he could find, knowing his life could well depend on the result, he twisted and pulled this way and strained the other way and wiggled and pushed. He managed to gain some purchase with his right hind paw on the edge of the rock holding him tightly. The strong claws gripped a crack in the rock just enough for him to be able to move forward. And he did, only slightly, but enough to break the rock's grip. His claws lost their grip and found it again. Ulysses twisted one way then the other all the while pushing with his powerful hind leg. Then in a breath, it was over. He was free. He shook himself and looked back at the arch. There staring at him, perfectly framed, was the puzzled fox. Ulysses lunged at him with a ferocious snarl and the fox was gone in an instant. Ulysses licked his genitals as if to get rid of any trace of the unwanted intruder who had, in fact, saved his life.

Ulysses stood for a long time looking at the smooth river and the meadow beyond. From time to time a branch would float past but he didn't pay much attention to how fast it was moving. Such was his desire to make the far shore. He shook himself once again and stepped into the river. The current picked him up immediately and swept him along. He was surprised at its speed and strength. He began to swim, and swim hard. He was making some headway but was dismayed to see his green meadow disappear as he sped by it. He was aiming for the far shore but was being carried down the river sideways at the mercy of the current. He continued to swim hard and made it to the middle of the river. He was tiring and realizing how difficult this crossing would be. His powerful four-legged strokes were making progress, and the shore was definitely looking closer. Then he heard the river's voice make a new sound. The river was roaring, and Ulysses was confused. He took his eyes off the far shore for a moment and looked downstream. He became more confused because his eyes told him that the river ended. It disappeared and all he could see was a wisp of mist where the river ought to be. The current quickened and the roar became deafening, and Ulysses found himself flung into the air with great force. Rolling and tumbling he fell into the mist. When suddenly, SMACK, all the air exploded from his lungs as he landed on his side at the foot of the falls. The roiling water quickly absorbed him and continued to tumble him underwater. He was utterly helpless and unable to breathe. A searing pain shot through his head as it hit a rock. He instinctively swam for the surface and his nose finally found it. The water was calmer, the current had slowed, and Ulysses was able to find his breath. He paddled just enough to keep his equilibrium while filling his lungs with sweet, fresh air. He became aware of a new sensation, something else he had never experienced before. He had swum in rivers and lakes many times and was always able to reach his destination. But something was wrong. The current was sweeping him in a big circle. Around and around. And the circle seemed to Ulysses to be getting ever smaller. Something told him to swim as hard as he could to the outer edge where the water was calmer. His head hurt and every muscle screamed for relief, but he swam as hard as he could. The strange current continued to pull him toward its center, and he knew that if it was successful it would mean his death. There would be no escape from the vortex. His survival instinct created a powerful response. When an organism is staring at its own imminent extinction strange forces come into play. The heart quickens to supply more blood to exhausted lactose-filled muscles. The body finds unknown reserves of adrenalin, and endorphins flow in abundance. The body has nothing to lose by performing beyond its maximum capacity because the alternative is its own annihilation. And so it was with Ulysses. He was beyond exhaustion but there was still the will. The will to swim. The will to survive. He swam with every bit of strength he had left until he felt like his heart would burst. But he knew he was making progress, and soon he found himself in the still water with the shore nearby, and the whirlpool behind him. He felt nothing in his body any more except the terrible ache in his head. Slowly, everything began to blur. His feet touched the pebbly shore. All sensation ebbed from his body until he lost all his senses, and everything went black.

CHAPTER 15

DIMITRI IS UNHAPPY

BERNARD SMOTE WAS FEEDING RAW MEAT TO HIS FISH WHEN HE WAS interrupted by the squawk of the international telephone. The domestic line sported a different sound, and his text phone a different sound yet again. He found this protocol gave him a brief moment to position his mind for the business about to unfold. This would be a call from his Russian client.

"Yes, Dimitri. How nice to…"

He listened for at least a minute, silent.

"Now Dimitri. You have no need to be upset, everything is going to be fine."

*

"Yes, yes, that's what I told you, and I will send you the Proof of Life photograph as soon as we have concluded our call."

*

"That's a very good question, Dimitri. I am reliably informed by my agent that the goods are currently in a clinic being prepared for international travel and…"

**

"Well, vaccinations, de-worming, ghastly things like that. And fleas too, I suppose…"

***

"No, no, Dimitri, please, I am not stalling. These things have to be done and…"

*

"Perhaps a week. There was some mention of a possible quarantine period and I am awaiting confirmation as to whether this is indeed necessary…"

Smote listened for another full minute, becoming more and more uneasy by the second, shifting his weight from one foot to the other.

"Dimitri, yes, I can tell you are angry because half your words are in Russian and you know I don't speak the language…"

****

"What?! No Dimitri, no. I beg you! There is no reason to cancel…"

**

"Really? Your mind is made up? Well, I must say Dimitri, I think you're being quite unreasonable. It's not like this is the first time we have done business. You were not satisfied with the Fabergé transaction? No one else could have gotten that for you. But I did."

*

"You're welcome. And the Edvard Munch?"

**

"Dimitri, please…"

Bernard Smote knew his client, and he knew that anything further would be pointless. He knew what was coming next.

"Of course, I will return your deposit, Yes I will."

**

"Yes, Dimitri. Good b—."

And the line went dead.

Initially, Smote was hurt. Hurt that a five-year relationship with Dimitri hadn't built up the kind of trusting equity he believed was there. He had clearly misjudged the man. He couldn't remember who proposed the adage, 'Never trust a Russian,' but it was certainly fitting in this case. His hurt was quickly replaced by anger. A deep dark anger directed at one Doctor Max Pfister, who had humiliated him with a good and long-standing client. And destroyed a profitable relationship. He picked up a phone from the table.

Text: *"Contract canceled. Demand immediate return first payment – 24 hours or consequences you and the animal."*

He disconnected, disinterested in anything Pfister might want to say. Smote clasped his hands behind his back and stared out the window and the park opposite and the walkers and joggers who knew nothing of the world he inhabited, and never would. And at some level, he envied them their innocence. He crossed the airy room to a small desk, and from the center drawer he removed a red leather Cartier address book. He had all the information on his computer of course, but sometimes yesterday's ways were preferable. The touch of fine grain leather would always be more pleasurable than that of a plastic keyboard. He picked up his domestic line, keyed in a number, and waited.

"Ah, Mr. Yurei…"

A fresh rain had just showered the campus at UC Davis. The sun now bore down, causing little puffs of steam to rise above the puddles.

As Max was drying his hands, he wondered why all institutional washrooms looked like they were designed by the architect's dry cleaner or a seven-year old child. Even he could do a better job than whoever imagined this sterile and boring space. His phone sounded. A text from Bernard Smote. He froze and stared at the reflection of a terrified one-eyed man in the mirror. His heart rate quickened. He leaned on the counter and made himself breathe deeply. He returned to his desk and, holding his head in his hands, forced himself to think. Max had the most serious problem of his life. This was an existential threat. Given the source, what else could 'consequences' mean? He didn't have the money to return, and just as important as his own mortality was the life of that magnificent animal that he had put in harm's way. How could someone be so stupid as to even think about destroying such an impressive and unique creature? After all, he had been planning the research necessary to genetically unlock the mysteries of this perfect life form. He would do a genome study as well, and the paper he would publish would be even better received than his thesis, "Super Dog – Genetic Planning to the Perfect Canine." That was a thesis after all, all theoretical. Now he would publish hard scientific results, and the worldwide academic community would know the name of Dr. Max Pfister. To hell with UC Davis. The big colleges and research facilities in the Ivy League universe would come calling. If his own survival were not enough, Max had an even greater motivation. To find Ulysses and save the dog's life.

And in the process find academic fame, and likely fortune, as well. He must find Ulysses before…

CHAPTER 16

MR. YUREI GETS AN ASSIGNMENT

THE DOUBLE GARAGE DOORS RESPONDED ONCE AGAIN TO THE remote-controlled signal, and they opened. The white Mercedes 600 Sedan rolled inside. Once closed, and not a moment before, a man emerged from the passenger's seat into the well-lit space. The car door closed automatically behind him with a heavy 'clunk.' He was a slight man in a brown suit wearing a nondescript tie against a plain white shirt. His shoes were just as unremarkable as the rest of his dress. Hisa appeared, bowed deeply, and beckoned the man to the stairs. Emerging into the room, his eyes took it all in as he was greeted by the man dressed all in white.

"Mr. Yurei. How lovely to see you again. Thank you for coming."

"It is always my pleasure."

"It's been what, a year since last we met?"

"Ten months, two and a half weeks, actually."

"Hisa, tea for our guest, and my usual, please. I believe the last time you were here you had the Keemun Black. Would that be your preference again?"

"Thank you, if you have it."

"Please, come and sit over here."

He directed his guest to one of the two Eames chairs separated by a low Danish teak coffee table. Once settled, Bernard Smote studied Mr. Yurei. If there was a single word to describe his appearance it would be 'plain.' If there was a noteworthy feature it would be his face, which was completely unnoteworthy. The man had a round, pleasant face with brown eyes and slightly pink cheeks. He was bald save for a ribbon of short-cropped hair that ran from behind one ear around to the other and down to his collar. In a crowd, even if he was noticed, he would likely be taken for an accountant or a music teacher. Mr. Yurei, a *nom de guerre*, of course, cultivated this look and found it an asset in his work. Being both unrecognizable and very forgettable suited his purpose. He was successful in his work because he was both invisible and because he had studied his craft well.

"Mr. Yurei, allow me to begin by telling you once again how satisfied I was with the results of your last commission. Your choice of a chemical that could not be detected even under autopsy was brilliant. The newspapers simply reported that the gentleman died 'of natural causes.' No trail to follow, no suspicion, case closed."

Hisa arrived with the tea and a glass of milk. He poured the tea from a dark red cast iron pot into a porcelain cup.

"I don't wish to pry, but I am curious. For you to successfully accomplish your task on Piccadilly in rush hour was masterful. So many people around. Do you mind sharing a trade secret or two with an admirer?"

The man held the teacup under his nose and inhaled. A slight smile crossed his lips.

"Tell me, what is the one item that most British men carry?"

"Other than a snobbish attitude, I can't imagine."

"An umbrella. The accessory no one notices. The umbrella I was carrying had a one-inch needle taped to its tip. The needle had been dipped in a chemical I chose, the name of which I am forbidden to mention. It is a very powerful and very illegal chemical, and it takes little to acquire the desired result. In the rush hour crowd, it was a simple matter really, for me to approach the subject from behind and jab him in the thigh. He might have felt the prick, but no matter. He took three steps, stumbled and fell, and was likely dead before he hit the pavement. Needless to say, a crowd gathered. Also, needless to say, I was not in it. On the corner where Shaftsbury Street joins Piccadilly Circus was a trash can. The only witness to the event was Eros, and I doubt he would say anything."

The man paused, lost in his recollection of the event.

"And I doubt they found the needle prick in his leg on autopsy. Far too small and not something the pathologist would look for."

There was a pause in the conversation as Hisa poured another cup of tea.

"That will be all for now, Hisa. Thank you."

Smote turned to face the other man.

"I have an assignment for you. But let me ask you a question before I go on."

The pleasant-looking man gave his host his full attention.

"Would you have any... concerns, if your target was an animal? A dog for instance?"

The man was expressionless, though a keen observer would have noticed that his eyes had hardened.

"Dogs, cats, chickens, horses, people – no matter. An assignment is an assignment."

"Good. Now allow me to give you some details."

And for the next 15 minutes he set out his arrangement with Max Pfister and the man's unusual behavior ever since he sent the Proof of Life picture. Further, Dr. Pfister had two hundred thousand of his dollars and had delivered nothing. But the real reason for this assignment was that the Bernard Smote's client in Moscow, impatient with what he considered a runaround, had canceled the contract. Pfister's actions had damaged Smote's reputation in the demimonde in which he did business. His integrity had been compromised and his honor besmirched.

"And no one does that to me! I want him and his prized dog gone. I would have no objection if you were able to stage the event so Pfister had to watch the animal die."

Mr. Yurei emptied his cup and stood up. He looked around the room. It was not quite as he remembered it. It probably meant nothing.

"Do you know where the contact is, or should I say, where the contacts are?"

"I have a strong sense they are not currently in the same place. There is something about Pfister's behavior that has made me very suspicious. I have written down for you the last known location of both. From there it's up to you. I recently transferred a significant sum of money to him for which he has provided no value. I believe I will be successful in reversing that transfer, however. It is sometimes useful to be a major shareholder in a certain bank in the Cayman Islands."

"That is your concern not mine. I will accept this assignment. It sounds like a nice change. Just to be clear, we will work on the same basis as the last time. That is, absolutely no contact until the assignment is successfully completed. And when that happens, I will notify you, and you will transfer funds in the same amount as last time, using the same banking coordinates. Do you agree?

"Yes, I agree."

The mild-mannered man stood and thrust his hands into the pockets of his brown jacket. He took a few paces this way and that. He stopped to address Smote directly.

"One of the reasons I am able to continue in my line of work is that I do not exist. In the field, I create a fictious identity complete with Social Security number, state driver's license, perhaps two, and two or three fully functioning credit cards in the name of a fictional person at a fictional address. This protects me of course, but my clients as well. In the unlikely event that something goes wrong, the client is completely insulated. If I don't exist, how could I possibly make or receive communications? I won't even have a phone with me."

Smote nodded. Impressed. Mr. Yurei continued.

"I think that concludes our business, does it not? Give me the last known contact information and I will leave you to your world of wonderful art and rare fish."

"Hisa. Hisa! Make the car ready, please."

Mr. Yurei's eyes scanned the room one last time.

"That's what it is! I knew there was something different."

"To what are you referring?" Smote asked impatiently.

"The vase. The Ming vase you told me so much about on my last visit. It's not here. Did you sell it? Surely you didn't sell it. It was clearly your favorite piece. And worth a fortune as I recall!"

Smote rose from his chair a little too quickly.

"Thank you for coming, Mr. Yurei. Hisa will see you to the car. Good day."

And with that he left the room.

CHAPTER 17

ULYSSES MEETS SOME UNUSUAL COMPANIONS

SOMETHING WAS LICKING HIS FACE. SOMETHING ELSE WAS LICKING at the blood near his ear. And something else was licking his ribs. Ulysses's head jerked up and he returned to consciousness quickly. He was confused and needed to orient himself. He was lying on a riverbank barely out of the water but on dry land – sort of. Standing around him were three sled dogs. His instinctive reaction was self-preservation, but Ulysses did not sense them to be aggressive. Quite the contrary. His three caregivers were anything but hostile. They were gentle and passive, and just stood there looking at him. One was light-colored and had a blue eye on one side and a brown one on the other. Another was beige with a white flash on its forehead and the third was darker and smaller than the other two. As Ulysses regained his senses, he tried to stand but was too weak, and he fell back. As best he could, he scented the three dogs and found them all to be female, and none in heat. They seemed very concerned for his welfare and tried to resume their therapeutic grooming. Ulysses didn't have the strength to object, and he let them minister to him without protest. Dusk was approaching and Ulysses desperately needed to be away from the river. He had had quite enough water for one day. For a lifetime perhaps. He was finally able to stand, and Blue Eye indicated with a glance over her shoulder that Ulysses should follow her. He was still very unsteady as the four of them slowly made their way into the thicket nearby where the dogs had their lair. Ulysses was nudged into it where he collapsed and quickly fell into a deep sleep. Probably the deepest of his life. It had been quite a day. Each of the dogs pointed her nose into the darkening skies and howled a primal howl, each in her own voice and each to her own melody.

This was a ritual they repeated nearly every evening until the next full moon. Ulysses's days were idyllic and his three companions always entertaining. The Little One was the most mischievous, chasing Ulysses through the woods, inviting him to catch her, staying just out of reach. Hiding, then circling around behind and nipping at his heels. Ulysses growled and feigned anger but very much enjoyed the play. White Flash was the most sober of the three and probably the eldest. She was the hunter and many an unfortunate rabbit or squirrel became the focus of a communal meal. It took Ulysses a full week to regain his strength, and his newfound home was so pleasurable that he fell into a daily routine of sleeping late, being groomed by his companions, having his food brought to him and generally enjoying the easy life. But as the moon waxed close to full, its mystical pull began to make him restless again and he knew he would have to leave this unlikely paradise soon. It had been many days since his feelings for his family had ached in his heart, such were the daily distractions. But he was changing, and the time to move on was approaching. His destiny was calling still.

Dawn the next morning was much like all the others as far as the dogs were concerned. White Flash had gone out to hunt before the others awoke; Blue Eye and Little One slowly roused themselves to greet the new day. But Ulysses acted differently and rebuffed their advances with a snarl. He ate the last of yesterday's kill and drank long at the little spring nearby. White Flash returned with a forest rabbit and while the dogs picked away at the carcass, Ulysses walked away from them. They stopped their eating and fixed him with their eyes, as if putting their lives in a state of suspension. Ulysses also stopped and looked back over his shoulder to meet their gaze. The four animals stood perfectly still in a moment of complete understanding. Ulysses turned and was soon devoured by the forest. As he threaded his way among the big cedars and pines to orient himself, he heard the howling. Three separate voices each singing her own distant lament.

CHAPTER 18

THE TRUCK

DUSK BROUGHT WITH IT A LIGHT DRIZZLE. ULYSSES WAS EXHAUSTED and his pace was slow. His head hung low, his ears were back, his fur was damp. The two-lane highway seemed endless and he had seen no signs of humans since the sun was high and warm. The only thing familiar was the scent of the pine forest, which the road had cut through for a very long time.

Ulysses knew he would have to stop soon. He also knew that the forest would provide shelter and food.

He stopped. He scented. He heard, his ears turning, first one then the other, to locate the sound.

It was behind him and it was a very big sound. A massive truck was slowing down. It had many lights and big metal bars over the front. It passed him as it slowed and Ulysses saw more wheels than he had ever seen, glistening in the rain. It rumbled to a stop and hissed and hissed, hurting his ears. Finally, it went silent except for the low growling rumble of its idling diesel engine. Ulysses watched, unsure, ready to disappear into the forest if danger came.

Though tired, wet and hungry, he was alert. The driver's door opened, and Ulysses saw a man step down from his very high seat. The man began to walk slowly toward him, but Ulysses sensed no danger, no aggression. As the man came closer, he was able to scent him.

Tobacco, coffee, sugar, meat, perspiration – but no fear. Ulysses could smell no fear in the man. He stood still, waiting.

"Well, look at you! All alone in the middle of nowhere."

The man stopped in front of Ulysses and knelt down on one knee. Ulysses smelled the leather in his boots mixed with an animal shit smell and gasoline. "It's 20K to the next sign of life and it will be dark in 30 minutes. Unless you really want to stay out here all night, you should come."

Ulysses and the man locked eyes. The man stood up.

"Come. Come on boy…" His voice was kind.

The man walked slowly away from Ulysses down the opposite side of the truck.

Passing seven double wheels, he stopped at the passenger's door. He reached up and opened it and stood quietly, inviting the dog to make a choice

"Come on, boy. It's OK. It's OK."

Ulysses had been on his own for the past four days and the human smells tumbling out of the cab wrapped in warm air somehow made him feel safe. Slowly he walked toward the man, looked at him, looked at the open door, and jumped up and into the truck.

"You're one smart puppy!"

The door slammed shut.

A moment later the man settled himself into his seat, snapped his seat belt into place and found a tune on the radio. Ulysses watched as his left hand released the airbrakes while his right grabbed a knob and selected a gear. His leather boots settled on the pedals. Ulysses heard the psh-psh of the air brakes being released and he picked up a slight oily smell. The big rig slowly began to move, and Ulysses heard the rhythmic rise and fall of the engine speed as the driver shifted through gear after gear on the way to cruising speed. While the man tended to his duties, Ulysses's eyes scanned the cabin. Open ashtray, a freshly crushed cigarette. More cigarettes in the box on the seat with a soft drink can beside them. Some pieces of paper on the dashboard and some stickers on the windshield glass. Nothing he saw or scented felt bad or threatening. Ulysses settled into his seat and, after checking the view through the windshield, he rested his head on his front paws. For the first time in many days he felt secure and, yes, comfortable.

Ulysses awoke with a start and a small bark. Steering with one hand, the man was carefully taking off his tight collar with the other, ruffling his fur gently. It took Ulysses a moment to recognize his surroundings.

"Whoa, sorry! Sorry. Hey, it's OK. It's all OK."

The man's voice was soothing and friendly and Ulysses felt that his hand meant no harm. The rhythmic rubbing was soothing in fact – something he had not felt in a very long time. When he was younger, Soleil and Akissuktok would rub him like that and it always felt good. Dan never did because he was always commanding and training and ordering. Even though Ulysses never received affection from Dan, he knew that deep down the man liked him. Ulysses always felt a strong, unspoken, connection with Dan.

Remembering his family made those terrible stirrings in his soul start again. They were always there just beneath his daily consciousness. Often, he was happier when he had to focus on survival and didn't have to feel those feelings. But now, as the big truck rumbled through the night, he was getting unsettled. Then the feelings slowly went away, as if they lacked the energy to stir him. He was just too tired. Too tired even to feel his spirit guide. The steady thrum of the engine and the quiet musical noise were all it took to get him to sleep. And he did.

CHAPTER 19

THE MINE

IT WAS THE SILENCE THAT ROUSED ULYSSES. AND HE AWOKE SHARPLY, all senses alert. He saw the inside of the cab of the truck and the scented the man beside him – both familiar and safe.

"We're here. I'm hungry. You?"

The keys jangled out of the ignition and into his pocket. The driver reached across Ulysses and released his door latch. Then he opened his own door and was lost from sight.

Ulysses pushed open the heavy door just enough for him to jump down. The truck had stopped in a large fenced industrial area. There were several cars and pickup trucks parked near a cluster of mobile buildings. They were are all dwarfed by two massive earth movers. Their wheels twice the height of a man; their yellow paint reflecting the soft morning sun. "Sunshine Mine – Copper for the World," and the number 19 painted on the closest door. The driver walked toward one of the trailer buildings, which identified itself by a sign above the door as "Canteen." And beneath it, a smaller sign in jaunty letters, "*The food may not be great, but there's lots of it!*" The driver entered with Ulysses close behind. The stove and refrigerator, both propane-powered, were at one end of the six-foot wide room. At the other were four small tables, two chairs at each separated by a serving counter. A small TV screen, which was off, was up in one corner, and a calendar with a picture of an open pit mine hung beneath it. Two very old faux oil paintings of forest lakes faced each other in the eating area vying for the title of worst grease-covered picture in the State of Montana.

A big, deep voice bellowed:

"The dog. OUT! C'mon Bernie, we got rules!"

The driver was taken aback and opened the door for Ulysses to leave.

"Rules? When'd that start?!

The big, deep voice returned to his griddle.

"Breakfast # 1? Home fries or beans? Whole wheat or rye? Toasted or plain? And where'd you find the dog…or the wolf…whatever it is?"

"I picked him up on the highway last night. Home fries please. He looked really beat. And rye. Once he got in the truck he slept straight through. Toasted. Butter and marmalade on the side."

"Coffee?"

"Does a bear shit in the woods?"

The cook cracked three eggs onto his smoky griddle and pushed around some already cooked bacon and sausages. Four slices of rye bread journeyed to the toaster.

"How'd you like to sell me a couple of naked hamburgers, Phil?"

The cook stopped mid-flip.

"What the fuck is a naked hamburger?"

"Don'cha remember that great scene in Five Easy Pieces? Remember Jack Nicholson is in this diner and all he wants is a side order of toast? And the bitch waitress says they got no side orders? Remember what he did next?"

"Yeah, sort of…no, not really."

"So, Jack Nicholson orders a chicken salad sandwich then tells the waitress to hold the chicken and hold the mayo and hold the lettuce and just give him the toast. She's pissed, and gets more pissed when Jack Nicholson tells her to hold the chicken between her knees!"

The cook let go a laugh that would have broken the windows if they weren't plexi.

"Yeah! Yeah! I remember now. He really nailed her!"

The toaster announced that the rye was ready for butter, with marmalade on the side.

The two men's hearty laughter evaporated into the air and there was quiet except for the greasy concerto playing out on the griddle. The chef plated Bernie's breakfast on a large oval platter and placed it on the serving counter with a new jar of Dundee Marmalade. He turned to get the coffee.

"So, like I said, what's a naked hamburger?"

Bernie broke the yolk of one of his eggs with a corner of rye toast and let it soak.

"OK, so you make hamburgers, right?"

"Is the Pope Catholic? Does a sailor's zipper get worn out on a Saturday night? Would a hooker…"

"OK! OK already! You need to get out more, Phil. You really do!"

Phil passed a very large mug of coffee over the counter.

"So, if I order a hamburger, what do I get with it?"

"Lettuce, tomato, onion and a piece of pickle on top of six ounces of good Alberta beef. Oh, and a bun lightly toasted on the griddle."

"Sounds great but here's what I want you to do. I'm going to order four hamburgers."

"What?! FOUR hamburgers?!"

"Phil, wait for it, Phil. Take a breath. So, I want four hamburgers. But, hold the lettuce, hold the tomato, hold the mayo and the pickle and hold the bun. Put the four patties on a plate and you don't even have to cook them – and you don't have to hold the bun between your knees."

Phil stared at his friend, who had apparently gone mad.

Bernie returned his gaze, slightly cocked his head toward the door and raised an eyebrow. Phil broke out into a big toothy grin.

"Well, fuck me sideways! I'll do you one better. I've got some chicken and bacon scraps that were going into the soup. I'll find something else for tomorrow's 'Cream of Yesterday.'"

Ulysses licked the plate clean as Bernie looked on. Phil came to the door and inhaled the welcome fresh air. He wiped his big hands on his small apron. He was uncharacteristically pensive.

"He's one hell of a beautiful animal, whatever he is. He's too big and well-

proportioned to be a wolf – and the white coat. He reminds me of something…Lemme think…"

"Well do it quickly will ya? Like a two-minute egg. I gotta be in Butte by tomorrow night – if you don't mind."

"A sled dog! That's it, he's like a really big sled dog. And it was only a couple of days ago that I seen this guy on the TV being interviewed. Some kind of a researcher or something. He said he was searching for one of his lab dogs who had run away, and it was big and white. Seems he had tracked it to not far from here."

"Well I sure would like to get this guy back to his rightful owner. He sure as hell isn't a stray. Do you think we could find this guy?"

"Shouldn't be too hard. I can call the TV station. They'll probably remember him."

"Why do you figure?"

"I don't guess they get to interview too many guys wearing a black eye patch."

CHAPTER 20

THE ROCKSLIDE

ULYSSES LEFT THE TWO MEN TALKING AND EXPLORED THE COMpound. There were no animal scents and only a few human. Mostly he smelled oil and diesel and grease, and he didn't like any of them. A few men in blue hard hats and yellow coveralls walked about. One got into a pickup and drove off. A diamond-shaped marker on the door announced, *'Danger – Explosives.'* Ulysses followed in the general direction of the truck, watched it turn to the right and drive out onto the vast expanse of the floor of an open pit mine. He had never seen anything man-made so big in his life. It was a huge, massive hole with steps and terraces banking hundreds of feet up to the original surface of the forest floor. There were three of the giant yellow earth movers on various terraces slowly moving their enormous loads up to the top. He watched the earth-clawing monster machine scoop up enough earth at one time to fill one of the yellow trucks full.

A warning sound — *"Whoop! Whoop!"* — caused every vehicle to stop its work. The operators stayed inside their machines. A PA system came to life.

"Ore blast in 60 seconds. Ore blast in 60 seconds."

"Whoop! Whoop!"

Ulysses turned away from the mine and ran along a hillside covered in low scrub brush. It badly needed a good rain.

In the distance he heard the PA again.

"Ten, nine, eight…"

He cocked his head unsure of what was going on.

"Three, two, one…"

"BOOOOMMMM!"

It wasn't the sound that alarmed Ulysses. It was the ground shaking under his feet. He had never experienced the earth not to be solid. Even with a snow blizzard blowing from every direction, the ground was always firm. The distant rumble soon became quiet but was replaced by a different, much closer sound, coming from the hillside right above him. He snapped his head around to look up the hill. Huge rocks, many, many of them, were rolling down the hill toward him. They clacked and cracked and rumbled and gathered speed. Some of the smaller ones were already pelting him painfully. He turned his eyes away and began to run down the hill away from the rocks. But they were rolling faster than he could run. They were catching him. A big one bounced off his right front paw. He yelped in pain. He saw blood. He tried to run but was swept up in the jumble of grinding, growling, dusty rocks. One struck the side of his head and everything went black.

His head ached and he tasted blood. Slowly his senses returned. He scented. But what? Something metallic? And water. He scented water. Then his ears picked up the slow drip-plunk, drip-plunk of waterdrops falling. But he could see nothing. Wherever he was, it was totally black. He found he was able to stand up, slowly, achingly, and he could move around several steps in every direction. But he was going by sound and smell and touch. Everything was totally and absolutely black. About as black as the feelings he was experiencing. It was not fear, like the

The Rockslide

fear of being confronted by a bear or a wild wolf. It was a more primal fear that told him his life was ending. He followed the sound of the dripping water and found a wet rock which he licked over and over again. Its cool wetness cleansed his mouth of the dust and blood. His foot hurt and his head hurt. And he was strangely tired. Or was he beginning to die? The air was clean and there was water. Something at least. Ulysses raised his head and a howl, which began in his belly twenty generations ago, flowed from his mouth into the blackness of the cave. He howled again. And he howled one last time. Then Ulysses laid down in his rocky tomb.

Ulysses found himself in a dreamworld. Or in the middle of a dream. Or in some other space and place all together. It was a world filled with images in black and white and every shade of gray he had ever seen. It was like the whole world had been put into a monochromatic kaleidoscope. He saw familiar images of trees and snow and Dan and sky and sun and Soleil and a river and an eagle – except there was no color. There was no pain in his body anymore and the blood on his foot had disappeared. He found himself floating through a world of floating images toward something, but he didn't know what. Then he began to see images he had never seen before. A fish ten times bigger than a salmon, an insect as wide as his paw with a thousand legs. Something that looked like a stick on the ground that slithered, a tiny red bird that hovered, and a huge gray animal with a little tail at one end and a bigger one at the other. He saw trees with big round balls at the top, and flowers of many different kinds, and he floated past bees and bugs and butterflies. He was going toward something, but what? And strangely, he was not afraid because despite all these new images he felt somehow a part of it all. He was one of them. They were all part of this magical realm. They were all a part of Nature. He knew he was a part of everything in the world that Nature created. He was at one with Nature. He was Nature.

His floating journey continued to unfold before him. On what looked like a distant horizon he began to see a shape. A large black shape that didn't look like any of the thousands of shapes he had passed by. It was almost round but not quite and it stayed in one place. And he knew it was alive. The shape slowly undulated and constantly changed. It was a huge dark primitive energy source. Like the middle of the sun. Only it was the blackest thing in this colourless world. It was the blackest thing Ulysses had ever seen. A different kind of black. A new kind of black. A blacker black. He floated toward the undulating figure and had no sense of its size. As he got closer, the surrounding images changed. He saw the births of hundreds of kinds of creatures from turtle eggs to whales to ants to humans to butterflies. And it was all beautiful. It was nature regenerating itself. It was all somehow – so right. But then he saw the death in nature. Death by aging until the creature didn't work anymore and simply stopped living. And death through extraordinary violence – or what Ulysses had come to know as violence. Was it Nature's normal way for a lion to gut a baby giraffe? Or for a praying mantis to decapitate its mate? Or for ten thousand krill to be swept up in the mouth of a humpback whale? Or a million honeybees to vanish? He saw the deaths of a hundred kinds of other creatures too. Ulysses continued his journey toward the black, black shape but seemed to get no closer to it. It wasn't that as he approached, it receded. It was, he realized, unattainable. Untouchable. Perfect in its own right. The perfect force. The Nature Mother from whom all things emanate. This was the Nature Mother.

Human voices and the sound of metal on rock brought him back to reality. He located the sound as being behind him and he turned

The Rockslide

toward it. For the first time he saw light. A pinprick of light where the sound was coming from dimly illuminated the cave, and Ulysses's keen eyesight registered a picture of his surroundings. Ulysses barked, three, four times. A voice in the distance cried out,

"He's in there. I tole ya!"

The metallic noise grew louder, and the light grew stronger. Ulysses struggled over slippery and irregular rocks, many of which fell away beneath his paws. As he got closer to the light, he scented fresh clean air and perspiration and iron. They smelled very good. He could see long metal rods probing, and the silhouettes of two men. They were straining with their pry bars against a large rock, which finally gave way. Sunlight poured into the cave and Ulysses bounded out and straight into the forest where he ran until his breath could carry him no more. Panting, he laid down on the mossy ground, felt the softness of the crunching leaves and smelled a wonderful mixture of decaying wood and the sweet muskiness of fresh black loam.

"Well, there's gratitude for ya!"

'He's got somewhere to go, Bernie."

"Yeah. Me too. Butte, remember? And no excuses if my drop-off is late."

"And this was…?"

"Just a little a landslide."

CHAPTER 21

ULYSSES REACQUAINTS WITH A FRIEND

ULYSSES SPENT THE NEXT TWO WEEKS TRAVELING NORTHEAST AND into northern Montana. Early on he encountered heavy forest, and the nights became cooler as he traversed Glacier National Park. He liked this kind of traveling because there were no people and food was plentiful. There was always a squirrel or a rabbit, and sometimes a lazy bird, too intent on pecking for grubs to be aware of his presence. He saw snow at the highest altitudes in the distance but chose to stay where there was food and running water. In the second week he sensed he was on the downhill side of the mountains as the air became warmer and the vegetation became thinner. Soon the foothills gave way to vast views of the Great Plains country, flat and brown as far as Ulysses could see. He skirted a small town appropriately named Cut Bank, cleaved in two by a river in a 150-foot gorge. He traveled mostly at night because there was nothing to conceal him during the day. He came to a major highway with the number 15 on it. Although he could make good time on the blacktop, he knew it was dangerous to be seen by passing motorists, so he spent a lot of time detouring into the brush on the shoulder when a vehicle came into sight or sound. Five dawns ago someone took a shot at him from a car as it sped by. The sound of the shot mixed with the sound of laughter had frightened him. Later in the day he passed a sign reading: 'Sweet Grass MT. Pop 6531' and a little farther down the road, 'The Sweet Grass – Coutts, Alberta Border Crossing. Prepare to Stop for Inspection.' The large, modern-looking building a mile down the road did not look good to Ulysses. It was open and naked, so he gave it a wide berth. The brown land in every direction was flat and empty and he had to travel far to avoid being seen. A small stream and a patch of green gave him welcome respite and he decided to stay there until dusk. With the crescent moon resting on the horizon of the darkening sky, he resumed his journey. Of course, he had no sense of when or where he crossed the border because a border is a human construct, meaningless to any of nature's creatures. Nothing looked different and nothing felt or smelled different, yet he was in Canada. His nature spirit with its unseen forces continued to orient him to the north. He traveled another hour when he was startled to hear a familiar human voice. He stopped in his tracks and scented – nothing – and scanned his surroundings. There, half a mile away, was a big tractor trailer idling by the side of the highway, its black diesel smoke smudging the evening sky. Following the custom's inspection, the driver had been pulling on the straps securing his cargo, but now he was waving at Ulysses and shouting.

"Hey Boy! BOY! Come! COME! What the hell are you doing here?!"

Ulysses recognized the man and his voice and ran to him without fear. They enjoyed an amiable reunion, and the man ruffled the fur around Ulysses's neck.

"Damn, what a coincidence. Hell, if they put something like this in a book, they wouldn't believe it!"

He ruffled the dog's fur again then wordlessly opened the passenger's door. He looked at Ulysses with a half-smile on his lips, Ulysses looked at him, looked at the door then back to him – and jumped up into the cab. The driver slid into his seat, slammed the door and released the air brakes.

"I got a long haul all the way to Edmonton. Just past Edmonton, actually. St. Albert is where I drop my load. That's about six hundred clicks and I could sure use the company."

The man and Ulysses locked eyes. He chuckled.

"Man, what are the odds?!"

He selected a gear, and the big rig strained up to speed. Ulysses sensed that this was a different cabin than the last time. The ashtray was closed and there were no cigarettes or food on the seat. It was cleaner, and all he could scent were the man and diesel fuel. And the leather from his boots, with no shit smell on them.

Approaching the same border crossing an hour later was a spotlessly clean black pickup with California plates driven by a man wearing an eyepatch. On the day after Ulysses escaped, Max had driven the 60 miles from Jackson, California to Sacramento and on to UC Davis. His face still hurt like hell, but his mind was clear, and he had gotten over the surprise and shock of the dog's escape. On the drive back to Davis he devised a plan to find Ulysses. He knew it would probably produce results slowly, but it was, at least, a plan. Using UC School of Veterinary Medicine letterhead, he wrote a press release from his office. He notified the reader that an animal involved in a Top Security Research Program had escaped from the facility. He described Ulysses in fine detail and provided contact information – which happened to be his personal cell phone number beneath his name followed by all his degrees, honorary and earned. He checked the United States Department of Agriculture website and found it was possible to send the press release to every USDA Veterinary Services Office west of the

Mississippi, with a single click. Which he did. He received his first hit within 12 hours from an office in the Redding District in California. He called to verify the report and ask if the animal had been captured. Only a sighting report, apparently. He thanked the young woman on the phone whose voice sounded like peppermint candy. If that was a good sighting and not some wolf or a vagrant white Pomeranian, it meant that Ulysses was traveling north as Max had hypothesized. Following two more sightings, one in central Idaho and one in the direction of the panhandle, Max gassed up the pickup and headed into the field. Nothing more from Benjamin Smote, which Max knew was bad. No news was definitely not good news and he didn't like the feeling. He had pulled his truck into the parking lot of the USDA Veterinary Services just north of Billings to confirm a sighting reported in the area. He always carried his almost authentic credentials from the university with him. They provided a certain authority to the reader and to himself. Max listened to the playback of the call-in. It sounded inconclusive, perhaps 60/40, but was worth pursuing. So, he returned to his truck and drove north on Route 87 toward Sweetgrass and in less than four hours was at the border crossing.

 At the Canadian Customs and Immigration side of the border, Max showed his passport and California Driver's License, and for good measure, his UC Davis credentials, which identified him as Doctor Pfister, a glaring oversight on the other two documents in his view.

 "And what is the purpose of your visit to Canada er… Doctor Pfister?"

 "Research."

 The Border Services officer looked at the documents carefully and handed them back.

 "Well, welcome to Canada, and have a good day."

In a brief minute he was on his way. Max's problem now was that he was out of the USDA's jurisdiction. Fortunately, he was also out of the jurisdiction of UC Davis in the unlikely event that someone had registered a complaint about his unauthorized press release. That was the least of his problems. He must find Ulysses before anybody else did. He had no option but to press on. He called up a map of Southeastern British Columbia and Manitoba on his iPad and studied it. He also called up a map of the Northwest Territories. Drawing a mental line between Yellowknife and Sweetgrass, the route Ulysses would likely take was clear. Edmonton was the highway gateway to the Northwest Territories and the road from Calgary to Edmonton was less than eight hours away. The fact the highway would first take him through Banff National Park and some of the most spectacular land in North America interested Max not in the least. He had no time for sightseeing. That was for tourists. He was on a life-and-death mission. His life or his death. The dog's life or the dog's death. He had to find that dog, and there was no way it was going to better him again. After all, he was the genius and the dog, was well, just, a dog.

Right?

CHAPTER 22

THE KID

ALTHOUGH HE COULDN'T KNOW IT, ULYSSES WAS IN NORTHERN Alberta. He loped along the tree-lined highway past a sign reading 'Island Lake 6 miles.' A cry in the forest stopped him in his tracks. He scented toward the sun – nothing. He scented in the other direction. He cocked his head, sounded and located the cry in the pine scrub. He ran toward it.

"Help! SHIT! Help!"

It was a young human sound. Running through the woods, he broke out into a campground with picnic tables, barbecue pits and two Porta Potties. A sign read: *"Welcome to the "Ole Swimin' Hole Campground."* A second sign nailed to a red post bearing a red-and-white life preserver ring warned, "DANGER. NO SWIMMING. SPRING FLOODING."

Ulysses ran past it to the riverbank where he saw a boy midway across a fallen tree that spanned the river. The angry water rushed over the log and across the boy's feet. He was frozen with fear.

"Help! Anybody!"

He saw Ulysses but was unable to move. Then the boy lost his footing, slipped and fell into the water but managed to grab onto a branch. The fast-moving current was trying to pull him away from the tree. The boy hung on as hard as he could. He realized that his life was in real danger. Ulysses turned to the life preserver ring. Stretching on his back legs he was able to knock it off its post and onto the ground. He grasped the rope attached to the ring in his mouth and dragged it toward the riverbank. Ulysses pushed his head through the life preserver ring and jumped into the river. It wasn't that different from his sled harness.

The boy's arms were just too tired. He couldn't hold on any longer. He lost his grip and the swirling water carried him away. The boy's only chance for survival was to grab the rope that the dog was dragging across the river. Ulysses swam with all his might toward the far shore, stretching the rope to its full length. The boy tried frantically to keep his head above water. Pool lessons don't come with a strong current. It swept him downstream – and right onto the rope. He grabbed it and hung on with all his might. Ulysses felt the weight of the boy and the drag of the current. With all his strength, Ulysses swam back toward the campsite. The dog's shoulders strained against the weight and the water. The familiar feeling of the sled dog harness, bred deep into him, gave him added strength. Determination in every stroke, he pulled on the life preserver ring. His progress measured in inches. Straining against the ring, the dog powered his precious human cargo toward to the shore. Ulysses finally reached the shore and the boy, though tiring, was still hanging on. Finally, the rope went slack. Ulysses ran back to the see the boy, exhausted but safe on the riverbank, leaning against a rock trying to catch his breath.

The boy and the dog looked at each other. The boy rubbed water from his face.

"Thanks and all that, but where's my backpack?"

Ulysses and the boy looked down river and saw it on the shore ten meters away.

"Maybe, if I'm lucky, there'll be some dry clothes inside. Fetch, boy, fetch!"

Ulysses sat still. Looked at him, then the backpack then to the boy again.

"Go Boy.! Fetch!"

Ulysses and the boy locked eyes. The dog didn't move a muscle.

"Dumb dog. I'll get it myself."

And Ulysses watched him do just that.

The contents of the backpack were wrapped in a green plastic bag and there were, in fact, some dry clothes. The boy struggled out of his wet jeans and into gray Gap sweats and a pair of mismatched socks. Next he pulled his soaking sweater over his head, revealing a training bra. Ulysses watched the transition intently.

"What are you staring at?!"

She quickly covered up with the matching top to the gray sweats, which had a hoodie. She squeezed water from her clothes and laid them out in the sun.

"Gonna need them tomorrow."

Ulysses turned his attention to the backpack lying on the ground. He nuzzled it open. He pulled out a plastic zip-lock bag containing some biscuits and carried it to his new friend.

"What, you hungry? Yeah me too, I guess. Thanks."

The Girl and the dog exchanged a look.

"My name's Luna. Yours? Aw crap! What am I doing talking to a *dog*?! I suppose you're hungry too, huh." She broke off a piece of biscuit and offered it to Ulysses, who turned his head aside.

"Here, eat," she persisted.

Ulysses turned his head aside again.

"OK, suit yourself."

She finished the biscuit and took a drink from a colorful water bottle with a butterfly on the side.

"How did you know I was hungry?"

She looked into Ulysses's deep brown eyes. They shared a moment.

"So, if you're so darn smart, what are we going to do next?"

It was getting dark and night sounds were everywhere. The air in the forest was still. It was like the wind was tired and taking a rest before its next tour of duty. Ulysses's eyes and nose scanned the air for signs of danger. Satisfied that they were safe he rested his head in his forepaws. Nearby, Luna lay curled up in the shelter of a tipped-up picnic table with her head on her backpack. She slept restlessly. Ulysses looked over at her, scented the air once again and, sensing no danger, settled down to sleep.

The next morning Ulysses awoke to find the girl snuggled into him. She stirred and slowly woke up, then became aware of her surroundings. She felt Ulysses body, was startled for a moment, then relaxed into his warm fur.

"This is summer. It's supposed to be warm. Brrr! Gotta pee."

She got up and walked toward a large tree, loosening the drawstring on her sweats. Ulysses stood up and looked at her. Luna returned his gaze, looked at the Porta Potty then back at him.

"Aw, you gotta be kidding!"

The dog barked.

"OK. OK. Geez, you're worse than prune-face Mrs. McIntyre."

Ulysses watched as she opened the door.

"Do you mind?!"

She closed and bolted the door.

Later, Luna went down to the riverbank, washed her face and brushed her teeth. She packed her brush, toothpaste and washcloth in a small red plastic zipper bag and stuffed it into her backpack. She hoisted it onto her shoulders.

"So, thanks and all that. I gotta be going, and I travel alone."

She started down the path toward the highway. Ulysses watched her go a few steps then began to follow.

"Go on, get lost! Beat it."

And she continued her journey. As they approached the highway, a red 10-year old GMC pickup sped by. The radio was loud, and a bag of garbage flew through the air narrowly missing the girl.

"Asshole!"

At the highway Luna started to walk toward the town, the same direction the pickup was traveling. Ulysses followed about 10 feet behind her. She spun around and walked sharply back toward the dog.

"Listen, I said get lost! OK? So, thanks for the river and all that but I would have made it OK on my own, right? So, beat it. I travel alone, remember?"

Ulysses took a step toward her.

"Back off mutt! I don't want you and I don't need you. I don't need *anybody* least of all a stupid dog! Now get lost!"

She glared at him until he finally turned and began to walk back into the woods.

Luna adjusted her backpack and resumed her journey to town. A tear ran down her cheek and she wiped her nose with the back of her hand. Then almost as a whisper, "I don't need anyone."

But the expression on her face said something else.

A few minutes later, the pickup reappeared driving on the other side of the road. As it neared the girl, it slowed.

"Hey kid, want a ride? Jump in, I'll take you into town."

"Naw, I'm good. Nice day for a walk."

The truck went into reverse and kept pace with her, driving backwards.

"C'mon, don't be stupid. Climb in the back if ya like."

"Hey, I said I was OK. Leave me alone."

The red truck pulled off on to the shoulder and the driver jammed it into Park. He jumped out and ran across the road. Luna saw him coming and started to run but he was too big and too fast.

"You're coming with me young lady. You're the one they're lookin' for and I aim to take you in – but not before you an' me get to know each other a little better."

He picked up the struggling girl under one arm and carried her toward the truck. She kicked and twisted but he was just too big. He carried her past the truck and down the shoulder into the brush.

"Yeah," he laughed, "we'll get to know each other just a little bit better."

Luna was thrown heavily to the ground and momentarily winded. The man took advantage of her stillness and began to pull at her sweats. They started to come down, revealing a pair of pink Joe Boxer shorts.

"Oooo," he leered, "my favourite color, pink. Come on little girl, you're gonna have a good time! We're gonna party!"

As the man reached for his belt, he was hit broadside by 120 pounds of snarling dog and slammed to the ground. Ulysses, his teeth bared, turned and stood over the frightened man. A guttural growl sounded deep in his throat. Powerless, the man could do nothing but wait to see what came next. Luna had fixed her clothes and she walked over to her prostrate attacker. She snap-kicked him flush in the groin. The man screamed in pain. Then she kicked him again, the first scream lost in the second.

"And one for good measure, you total scumbag. You want to try something stupid again? You'll have to deal with me and my bodyguard."

Ulysses and Luna left the man writhing in pain among the fallen pine needles. She headed back to the highway and past the red pickup toward the town. As they walked past the truck Ulysses stopped and looked through the open door.

"What!" she said impatiently.

The girl peered into the cab and saw the dangling car keys.

"Great idea!"

She took them and threw them as far as she could into the scrub on the other side of the road.

"Asshole!"

Luna, now with a friend, resumed her journey. The man stood up, slightly bent over, and leaned on the trunk of a big pine. He groaned as he started to take a few steps up the road shoulder to his truck. He found his cell on the front seat and punched in a number.

"Hey Andy. Marty here. You know that wolf with the bounty on it? Yeah, well listen, I just seen it. He even attacked me! Me? I'm OK – sorta. Listen, get Jake and load up. We're goin' on a wolf hunt. How're we gonna find him? Not a problem. I know where's he's going. It'll be like shooting fish in a barrel with a two-grand payout at the end. Later."

Three out-of-work miners embarking on a lethal mission. He pressed End and threw the cell back on the seat. The man reached for the ignition.

"Why you little bitch!"

His hand went under the dashboard and pulled hard at some unseen wires.

"It's gonna take more than that to stop me, little miss."

Working by touch alone he manipulated the wires and the starter connected. The big V-8 barked to life.

"How do ya think I got this truck in the first place?!"

The man slammed the gearshift into drive and tromped the gas. The truck did a noisy U-turn, throwing gravel and leaving a strip of black on the highway. It accelerated down the road and was lost around a corner in seconds.

The only witnesses to these events were a big old vulture picking at a piece of roadkill, and the impersonal, uncaring forest.

And Max Pfister, standing behind one of the last-remaining 100-year-old Red Cedars in the country.

CHAPTER 23

THE KID FINDS A FRIEND

ULYSSES AND LUNA APPROACHED THE SMALL LAYOVER CAMPground made up of three picnic tables, a barbecue pit and a Porta Potty.

"Let's stop here a minute. I gotta do something."

Ulysses looked at the Porta Potty.

"No! Geez ! Not that."

She unzipped her backpack and pulled out the clothes she had been wearing the previous day, now dried, and a black baseball cap with the number 5 in Roman numerals on the front.

"Just gimme a minute, OK?"

She disappeared behind the Porta Potty, emerging moments later in yesterday's clothes. She put the baseball cap on her head, backwards of course, but not before tucking in a few strands of her already short black hair. Ulysses watched the transformation, not knowing it was about to get even more interesting. Luna tugged at her sweatshirt then moved her shoulders back and forth. She walked toward Ulysses with a different kind of walk. Ulysses cocked his head to the side. Her arms swung differently too. She stopped in front the dog.

"Well, whaddya think?"

Ulysses was puzzled because she didn't sound like the girl he had just been with. Her voice was pitched lower and she spoke slower.

"I get that it's probably kinda weird to you, but believe me, it's better traveling alone being a boy," she said in a boy's voice.

He cleared his throat.

"Ahem. Hi, my name is Lucas and I'm takin' a trip."

Ulysses looked at him, then down to the ground and back to him. He cocked his head.

"Well, how do I sound? Yeah right, like you are about to tell me. Okay, let's get into town. I could use a sandwich and a soda."

Lucas repacked his backpack and they left the campsite. It didn't take them long to reach the town. Well, almost a town if you can call five or six stores and as many houses a town. While Ulysses waited outside, Lucas went into the General Store and returned shortly with a homemade egg salad sandwich, an orange soda and a butter tart. At the end of the building, the owners had put out two tables with four plastic chairs each. One of the chairs was occupied by a young boy who was also enjoying an egg salad sandwich. The two boys glanced at each other as Ulysses and his companion took the other table. Lucas pulled the plastic wrap from his sandwich and popped the tab on his soda. They all sat there in an uneasy silence. Finally, the other boy spoke.

"Pretty good sandwich, right? You can't beat homemade. They probably have the chickens it came from."

"Yeah, it's good."

"My name's Dylan. Your dog?"

"Sort of. Well, not really. We just met yesterday, actually. I'm Lucas."

"Man, he's big!"

"Strong too. You wouldn't want to get on his bad side."

Ulysses watched the awkward conversation, looking from one boy to the other and back. Lucas continued.

"So, what are you like doing here? It's like, the middle of nowhere."

Dylan gestured to a very large backpack with aluminum tent poles protruding from the top. Sixty liters capacity at least.

"I'm on a sort of camping, hiking, hitchhiking sort of a trip. I have been on the road for four days now. There are lots of campsites along this highway – tourists, you know – but it's been slow because I'm doing a lot of walking. I'm pretty nervous about actually hitchhiking, you know? Sometimes a family will stop and if it feels OK, I'll take the ride. But…"

"Yeah, I do know. I get it. It can be scary."

Ulysses laid down beside Dylan's backpack. The boys finished their sandwiches and Lucas started on his butter tart. He picked up the conversation, which was becoming easier and easier.

"So, where are you headed for?"

"Just south of Edmonton," Dylan said. "I have an uncle and an aunt there. Place called Pigeon Lake. But I've got a ways to go because we're north of Edmonton now, right? I think Athabasca is down the road. Maybe twenty-five miles. You?"

"Yeah, well, I'm going north. Maybe to Yellowknife, I think."

"Whoa! That's a way longer trip than mine! Like, what's up there?"

"I don't really want to talk about it right now."

"Yeah, sure. No worries. No pressure."

Ulysses and Lucas watched as Dylan collected up all the wrappers and took them to the trash. Then he hauled his backpack onto his back, shrugged it into place and hooked his thumbs under the shoulder straps.

"It's been great talking to you and I sure wish you luck with your huge trip."

"Yeah, you too. Say hi to your aunt and uncle for me."

Dylan turned and started down the road, then stopped.

"You know, this may sound crazy, and I don't want you to think I'm weird or anything, but, like…you wouldn't want to travel together, would you? I mean at least until we get to Edmonton? I mean, you don't have to if you don't want…Yeah, probably not…"

"No! That's great! Sure, I'm up for that. Makes sense. A whole lot safer hitching when there's two of you, right?

"Besides, you'll have your dog with you. I'm not exactly sure how that will affect our hitchhiking chances, but we can talk about that tonight."

Dylan took out his iPhone and tapped on the screen.

"It says there's a good overnight campsite only about two miles along that sideroad there, and we can walk that easily. Do you think maybe we should pick up a little extra food before we head out? You know, the dog and all…?"

And that's what they did. They also picked up some more bug-spray and toilet paper. Half an hour later the campsite came into view about 50 yards off the road. They turned into it and Dylan picked out a location for the tent. It was beside a big tree, and flat, and obviously had been used many times before, meaning no bumps under the blanket. The yellow and green tent was a snug two-person model with zipper entrances front and back. The boys had it pitched in 10 minutes – a new procedure for Lucas, a familiar one to Dylan. In the absence of a proper blanket, Lucas figured he would put on his extra sweatshirt if it got cold. As this was happening, Ulysses wandered off into the wood to do some exploring of his own.

When he returned three hours later, the boys were just finishing dinner. They had collected wood and lit it in the stone barbecue. The metal rack had seen better days, but it held the hot dogs and buns. Ulysses saw that they were talking easily and were obviously

The Kid Finds a Friend

comfortable in each other's company. Lucas found a grassy place to scoop out Ulysses's tinned food. Half a tin tonight and half in the morning. During dinner, dusk fell, and the fire died down. The bugs came out, but they didn't spoil the moment, and good old-fashioned hot dogs had never tasted better. As darkness fell, they cleaned up the campsite. Dylan saw that there were stout six-inch nails in the tree they were under, about eight feet up. He hung his backpack up there and suggested that Lucas do the same.

"Bears. They probably won't come around because we're sorta close to the highway but better safe than sorry. There's blacks around here and they only grow to about 350 pounds, so this should make us bear-proof."

Lucas was taking all this in, unsure.

"Unless, of course, a Grizzly comes by, then that's way different."

"WHAT?! A Grizzly?!"

"Kidding! Just kidding. No Grizzlies this far south."

"That wasn't funny."

And Lucas punched Dylan in the arm. With a pat on the head for Ulysses, and a little awkwardness, the two boys got into the tent and did up the zippers. Dylan turned on a small LED flashlight and pointed it to the top of the tent. It created a soft and warm half-light. He gave the tent a quick burst of bug-spray and settled down under his blanket. Lucas stared at the ceiling feeling slightly ill at ease. He sensed that Dylan felt the same. Dylan broke the silence.

"Like I don't want to be like nosey, but how come you're going to Yellowknife? I mean, if it's private, that's OK, I understa—"

"It's not like that. Have you ever wished for something so hard that you feel like if you don't get it you'll just die? I mean the disappointment would be like terminal? And if you talk about it too much it'll make it not happen. Like a curse? Like that?"

"Well, yeah, sort of… I guess…"

"I have never told this to another living soul, not to mention someone I met four hours ago, but I have a sister, and I really, really love her and I really, really need to find her."

"What do you mean 'find her.' Don't you know where she lives?"

"Well, not exactly."

"Come on, dude. What does that mean? 'Not exactly'?"

"I mean, I think she might be in Yellowknife."

"How do you know that?"

"Never mind. And I'm sorry I mentioned it. Forget it. You wouldn't understand."

"Hey chill. Maybe I will understand – if you give me a chance."

Lucas was still and quiet for a full five minutes. To his credit, Dylan respected the silence and sensed that this was an important moment for his newfound friend. A newfound friend who, the more time they spent together, made him feel… strange. Dylan couldn't put his finger on it but there was something… different about Lucas, who then broke the silence.

"My sister and I were in a foster home and there were other kids there too. The man and his wife were raking in the money from Social Services and we sure didn't get much benefit from it. They were really mean and way more strict than they needed to be. My sister got kicked out when she was eighteen. I was too young and I had to stay. We knew she had to go, but it really bummed me out because she was my bestest friend ever. She told me she thought maybe we had some cousins around Yellowknife and that's where she would try to get to.

The Kid Finds a Friend

Our parents used to live up there when we were really young. Maybe they were Dene. I dunno really."

Lucas went quiet again as if struggling to recall those normal, happy times from many years ago.

"Anyway, I stuck it out for a long time until I couldn't anymore, and last week I ran away. I figured they would probably put out an Amber Alert for me, then I figured they probably wouldn't because they would lose the money from Social Services, who hardly ever came to the house to check on us or anything, so they wouldn't even know I was gone. And the money would keep coming in."

Lucas was fighting to hold back tears, something that mustn't happen in front of Dylan.

"I really miss my sister. I really miss her…"

Lucas bit down on his tongue and it hurt like hell. Finally, he could hold it in no longer and he broke down into deep shoulder-shaking sobs. Gone was the young man's voice as a little, frightened lonely girl cried her heart out. Dylan sat stunned, the emotions filling their little tent. Not knowing what to do, he unzipped the tent flap thinking that the girl might take some comfort from the presence of Ulysses. Which she did, and slowly her jerky breathing became deep and regular again. She tore off three feet of toilet paper and scrunched it into a ball to mop her eyes and blow her nose. They both left the tent and stood in the night. Dylan reached out to her and touched her arm.

"I know we don't know each other… but could I give you a hug? But only if you want to…"

Lucas folded into Dylan's arms and the tears almost began again. They separated and Dylan looked her full in the face.

"So, what's your real name?"

She swallowed hard and bit at her fingernail.

"Luna. My name is Luna."

Dylan exploded into a little dance and he spun round and round. The woods echoed with his shouts.

"WOO HOO! Totally amazing! Woo HOO!! This is way, way, too amazing!"

Luna was totally confused as Dylan burst out into laughter. Total, uncontrolled laughter.

"What's so funny? I think Luna is a pretty name. I like it."

"No, no, it's not that at all. It's a beautiful name. In fact, a very beautiful name. Maybe the most beautiful name I have ever heard! You have just saved my life!"

"Wha…What are you talking about??"

Dylan led Luna to the picnic bench and sat her down. He took a deep breath.

"You were really brave tonight telling me your story. That took a lot of courage and I really respect you for that. But I have a secret for you too, and you have to promise not to say anything until I'm finished. Right? OK?"

Luna nodded slowly, more than a little unsure of what was about to happen.

"So, when we met today, I thought you were an OK guy. We're about the same age give or take a year or so, right? And you're a little smaller than me, but you seemed like an OK guy. But then, and here's the secret, and it's really weird, I started to get…like feelings for you! It was crazy. We had just met, I have never had any kind of feelings for another guy in my entire life, but here I was having feelings for you! I was thinking that maybe I'm a perv. Or a closet gay guy and I don't know it yet. Or bisexual. Or just weird. And the more time I spent with you the stronger my feelings got. And the more crazy and confused I

The Kid Finds a Friend

felt. And when we were in the tent getting ready to go to sleep before we started talking, I actually had…well, I actually got…a boner! I was going quietly nuts right up until you started to cry, and you were crying like a girl and then I knew you were a girl. And when you told me your name was Luna, you actually saved my life. You're a girl, I'm a guy, and it's all good!"

"That must have been really tough for you. I am sorry. I lied to you, but I sort of had to, right?"

"Absolutely you had to, and you have nothing to be sorry for."

A night bird called out, another replied, and the wind rustled the treetops.

"Do you think we might be able to get some sleep now?"

"Yeah, I think so. Actually, I'm sure so."

So, with a ruffle of Ulysses's fur, they returned to the tent and zipped themselves in. They lay quietly, each lost in their own thoughts and feelings. It had been quite a night.

"Good night Dylan. You're really a nice guy."

"And the same to you, Luna. Oh, one more thing."

"Yes?"

"What is your sister's name?"

Luna took a deep breath.

"Soleil. Her name is Soleil."

The next morning, Ulysses was nowhere to be seen. Luna called out to the dog at the top of her lungs but with no result. Dylan could see she was concerned.

"You know, he probably has somewhere to go too. Don't be sad. Who knows, you may hook up again sometime. C'mon. We have to hit the road."

They collapsed and packed the tent in five minutes, shared a small box of Rice Krispies and an apple and, after cleaning up the campsite, shouldered their backpacks and struck off in the direction of the main highway.

CHAPTER 24

ULYSSES'S UNEXPECTED EVENT

ULYSSES WAS BACK ON THE TWO-LANE BLACKTOP NEAR THE grocery store. He sensed that Luna would be safe with Dylan, who would look out for her and they would travel well together. He was having difficulty orienting himself in the overcast day with no sun to guide him. Scenting and listening, all he heard was the raucous caw of a big crow filling the forest with its obstinate sound. As he headed north along the shoulder of the highway, he walked past a sign bearing a tied garbage bag icon and the words "Town Dump" and "Beware of Bears." He ignored the entrance, and just past the sign he saw a small roadway running off to the east. He scented and oriented and began to walk down it. The crow squawked again, and a breeze ruffled the topmost branches of the trees.

BANG! A shot rang out! Ulysses was blown over! He had been shot!

"Woo hoo! Ya got him! Good shot Marty."

"So, one of youse guys finish him off while I go get the pickup. We can throw him in the back and go collect our two grand!"

The three men scurried out of their hiding place. Two of them ran to the red pickup hidden out of sight, while the third ran toward the helpless animal. The bullet had smashed into Ulysses's right shoulder. There was already a lot of blood seeping onto his white fur. He was lying on his left side, panting fast and unable to move. The three men arrived at the scene, breathless, excited and drunk. Marty cocked his Winchester. At that moment a very big, very black and very new pickup made a fast turn into the laneway and came to a locked-wheel dust-throwing stop. The three men stood frozen as a tall man wearing a long black coat and a black drover's hat jumped out of truck screaming.

"You've shot my dog, you subthalamic cretins!"

He knelt to examine Ulysses's shoulder.

"Son-of-a-bitch! What have you done?!"

Max ran to the back of his truck and brought a large, flattened canvas sack to lay beside the stricken animal. As gently as he could he slid Ulysses onto it.

"Now, you idiots pick that up with as much care as your pea brains can muster and bring it over to my truck. If I hear as much as a whimper out of my dog the RCMP will have your asses for dinner."

They put Ulysses into the pickup and Max clanged the tailgate shut. He jumped in and wheeled the vehicle around and back on to the highway. The three men could do nothing but stand there and try to understand what had just happened.

"Wonder what happened to his other eye?"

"What's a South Atlantic cretin?"

"I don't feel too good."

And he puked flat beer and soggy nacho chips onto the boots of the other two men.

The black pickup turned fast into the motel parking lot. It backed into the spot directly in front of unit 107 where Max unlocked the door and propped it open with a chair. With great effort and even greater care he slid his arms under Ulysses and struggled to carry the 120-pound dog inside. Perspiration beading his forehead, Max placed him on the unused bed. He let out a long deep breath, locked the door and took off his hat and his coat, hanging them on the hook behind the door. He turned his attention to Ulysses, whose rapid and shallow breathing told him the dog's condition was serious. He looked in the dog's eyes and saw pupil response and then checked his tongue – it was still moist. Good. From across the room he retrieved a small square, hardcover case and snapped it open. He took out a syringe with a 5-millimeter needle, which he inserted into a phial. He withdrew 4cc of the clear liquid and, feeling for the muscles between Ulysses's shoulder blades, inserted the needle and depressed the plunger. He looked again into Ulysses's eyes, but this time with compassion and caring. He stroked his ribs and flank gently over and over again. His voice was soft, almost inaudible.

"That will relax you, my beautiful boy. That bullet has to come out."

Ulysses scented that this was the same man who had taken him on the dreadful long journey many months ago. He felt fear. But he didn't smell fear or aggression from the man. Ulysses felt pain like he had never experienced in his life, and he could not move. He struggled to catch his breath. Slowly a strange feeling began to wash over the insides of his body as his muscles began to relax. It was a pleasant feeling. Warm. Soothing. His eyes lost their focus and he couldn't scent any more except for a strange sweet smell. The same sweet smell he remembered from the night he was forced into the canvas bag before the race was supposed to start. He... felt... strange... and he started drifting... Scattered visions floated through his mind. He saw Dan chopping wood. He saw Soleil feeding him from the baby's bottle and cuddling him to her soft breast. He remembered the distinctive taste of Soleil's milk and could almost taste it now. And he saw the baby Akkis, secure and smiling in her beaded cradleboard. Then his visions became darker and he was in the world of the Nature Mother again with its images of death and suffering. It all began to slowly spin, and…

Max tore a pillowcase open into a single piece of cloth. With a pair of surgical scissors from his black case, he cut a hole six inches in diameter. Ulysses's entire body was covered by the white cloth except for the bloody wound. Max pulled the small desk closer to his chair and focused the reading lamp onto his working area. He took a pair of surgical forceps out of the case and inserted them very slowly into the wound.

"I hope to God it didn't shatter a rib," he whispered.

It was as close as Max had come to a prayer in 20 years. The last time he had acknowledged a Higher Power was five years ago when he cursed Him from the depth of his being for taking away the sight in his right eye and allowing his beloved Thorne to be killed. He still hadn't forgiven Him and had remained a steadfastly bitter man. It was as if someone had reached into his soul and taken out all the human parts. And it was all His fault. Max returned his attention to the wounded dog. Steadily and surely the tip of the forceps went deeper into the wound. Almost imperceptibly, Max probed for some contact. If the entry wound was much deeper, it would mean that the bullet had penetrated the rib cage and was lodged somewhere beneath it in the soft tissue there. And that soft tissue was made of lung and heart and large blood vessels. He probed even deeper.

"Were doing fine here, my boy. Just fine…"

He tried to visualize the blood-covered forceps in the channel of the wound as they searched very slowly and carefully in the red darkness for something that didn't belong there. Max's hand stopped. He was completely motionless. He had felt rather than heard the tiniest 'click' as the forceps touched the foreign metal in Ulysses's body.

"There you are you malignant bastard. I got you. And you are where you should be – on the right side of his ribs."

Turning the forceps slowly and carefully opening the jaws, Max was able to grip the bullet with a snap of the rachet in the handle. Steadily and surely, he withdrew the forceps, released the rachet, and the bloody bullet dropped into the ashtray on the small desk with a glassy 'clink.' He let out a long breath and wiped his forehead with his sleeve.

"That's a good start. Now some sulfa powder, and what you need most right now, sleep."

He applied the powder generously and cleaned much of the dried blood from around the wound. There was nothing more he could do now except remove the pillowcase sheet and dim the lights in the room. He looked down at the mighty creature, now just a weak and helpless animal. Max laid down on the bed beside Ulysses and stroked Ulysses's back and buried his face in the fur of his neck. His voice was a whisper.

"That's my good boy. That's my beautiful boy. My beautiful boy…"

He felt the shape of Ulysses body as it melded to his own. It radiated a sensual warmth.

Max stayed there for a long time. And as he did, a melody from the seventh madrigal in the *'Lagrime de San Pietro'* came to his mind and he hummed it quietly into the dog's ear. Though originally written as a lament to Saint Peter, Max felt that the timeless beauty of this Renaissance music would somehow strengthen his ailing dog, while bringing a sense of peace to him. There was something spiritual about the human voice singing acapella. And Max was sensing something unusual in his feelings for this dog.

Max was unsure how long he slept. A quick check of the red numbers of the digital bedside clock revealed 7:44 p.m. He raised himself up on one elbow and looked down at Ulysses. He was still asleep and would be all right until the morning when he would need fresh antibiotics, water and possibly some food. As he got up, a change came over the man. He hardened as if his earlier feelings had been a mistake.

"I have got you now. You are mine again," spoke a voice with an edge.

To his surprise, Max found that he was hungry, and fortunately, the motel had a small restaurant. Although he felt that referring to the motel's eating facility as a 'restaurant' was somewhat optimistic, he was fairly certain he could find something on the menu that they couldn't ruin. He pulled the bedcover over Ulysses, picked up his current book, a biography of Leonardo DaVinci, locked the door and walked to the restaurant just as the lights in the parking area went on. He had no reason to notice the dark green late model sedan with the Hertz sticker on the rear-view mirror sitting unobtrusively in the corner of the lot, or the man inside it. As he opened the door, he made a mental note to contact Dr. Swanson at UC Davis, to make sure his booking in the lab for tests for Ulysses was still OK even though the schedule had changed. After all, he had put down a deposit, and his money was as good as anyone else's.

CHAPTER 25

MAX'S SURPRISE ENCOUNTER

"And will that be with home fries or mash, hon?"

"Home fries."

The server called over her shoulder.

"Johnny, a Number 3 at home."

"And a coffee, black, while I am waiting, please."

Max took out his phone. No incoming. He let out a long breath as his coffee arrived with four creamers. He pushed them aside and shook his head.

Focusing on his phone, he didn't see the balding man with a pleasant, round face enter the restaurant. No one did. He was that kind of person. He paused to take in the place.

"Dinner, dearie?"

"Oh, I think all I will have time for is a piece of your wonderful apple pie and a glass of milk if that's OK with you."

"No problem. Right this way."

The server led the man toward a table just beyond where Max was seated. As the man passed by, he stumbled and brushed against Max's table, jostling his coffee. From a small plastic bottle in the palm of his hand, about half the size of a cigarette, a clear liquid squirted out, much of it onto the table but some went into the mug.

"Oh, golly mister. I'm really sorry, I'm so dang clumsy sometimes."

"You should watch where you are going!"

Max returned his attention to his phone. Nothing. His meal arrived, and the server wiped up the spilled coffee. Max had reasoned that they couldn't mess up scrambled eggs with crisp bacon and whole wheat toast and jam. He was wrong. He sipped his coffee, puzzled by the lack of response from his phone. He opened his book at Chapter 11, *"Bees and Flight,"* and began to read, oblivious to the food he was eating.

"More coffee, hon?"

"No, I'm fine. Bring the check, will you?"

The man at the next table gestured to the server.

"Excuse me, miss, where is the… ah…you know…"

"Just past the front door on your right."

"Oh, thank you so much."

No one noticed that the man quietly turned left and went out the front door.

Max looked at his phone again and blinked. The screen was in soft focus. And he was feeling distinctly – odd. He shook his head and noticed that he was having difficulty catching his breath. He couldn't focus. As his symptoms worsened his training told him what was happening to him. He had been poisoned.

"Here's your check, dearie. Say, you don't look too good. You OK?"

Max's speech became labored.

"Charcoal. Get me sharcoal fr'm th' grill! NOW!"

Saliva filled his mouth and his lips became flecked with bubbled spittle. His uncovered eye went wide.

"The daw…the doggg…"

Mac fell unconscious to the floor, his body quivering, his breath gurgling and labored.

Max's Surprise Encounter

The server and the cook stood riveted to the spot staring at the dying man. One of the other diners jumped up.

"The best bet is the clinic up at Athabasca University. It's a small facility but it's only 12 miles away. You call them and tell them an emergency is coming in, and Elaine and I will drive him there. Quicker than an ambulance from the city. I don't know what this is. It's not a heart attack but it looks really serious. We gotta get moving. And call the RCMP."

The station wagon raced through the twilight and in a few minutes arrived at its destination. There were two office workers and a First Nations security guard waiting with a wheelchair. They put the unconscious man into it. The young security guard stared at Max.

"I've seen this before. I think it's poison."

"Poison! Oh my God. What are we going to do?" cried the younger of the two office workers.

"The Northern Wellness Conference dinner is just breaking up," said the other, "and one of the speakers is a Healer. I heard her speak. Quick, take the man to the clinic and put on an oxygen mask. I'll go and find the Healer."

As they hurriedly pushed the wheelchair down the hall the younger woman asked,

"Do you remember the Healer's name?"

"Ah...let me think." She paused. "Yes, her name is Soleil. She came down from Yellowknife. She gave a paper on the dangers of arsenic in mine-tailing ponds."

Soleil hurried into the small one-bed clinic room. She stopped in her tracks and stared down at the quivering Max Pfister. With a calm that belied her inner turmoil she turned to the security guard.

"Get me the following plants from your home or from the reservation store. And get them fast! And add these last three items."

She handed the young man the hastily scribbled list. He ran out the door, leaving the two office workers.

"Try and contact Dr. Tall Pine and tell him we have a poisoning case here, and it is serious. He is in Yellowknife. There's nothing the two of you can do here so you should probably leave him with me."

And there was little Soleil could do until her remedies were delivered. She loosened Max's clothing and adjusted the oxygen mask. She stared down at the one-eyed man on the threshold of death. This man who no one liked and who many believed was behind Ulysses's disappearance last winter. Soleil remembered him for his visits two years apart when he tried to buy Ulysses, but Dan was having no part of it. This one-eyed person was a rude man, an unpleasant man and neither she nor Dan liked him. But Soleil could not hold anger or hatred in her heart now for a man struggling for his life. And she pushed those thoughts and feelings aside.

She sat cross-legged on the floor beside the narrow bed and took Max's hand and pressed it to her forehead. After a full minute of stillness, she began to rock back and forth, forth and back. A quiet chant parted her lips and the sound of an ancient healing song filled the room. The music came from deep in her belly and deeper in her history.

Max stirred. His sighted eye opened but saw nothing. In his delirium, his other hand tore at the oxygen mask.

"The daw…The do…"

And he lapsed into unconsciousness again. Soleil took the man's hand from her forehead and held it very tightly in both her hands.

"Sante nan mwen ap koule tankou dlo nan ou,
Sante nan mwen ap koule tankou dlo nan ou."

(Health through me is flowing into you).

And rocking back and forth she continued the incantation in a barely audible voice.

"*Sante nan mwen ap koule tankou dlo nan ou,*
Sante nan mwen ap koule tankou dlo nan ou."

Her quiet chant was interrupted by the sound of the door opening. The breathless security guard handed her a small box decorated in porcupine quills and beads. She looked up, questioning.

"Everything you asked for. The Elders want you to know they are praying with you for the soul of the man."

The young man watched intently as Soleil opened the box and examined the grasses, petals and roots. She raised the rich-smelling mixture to her nose and breathed in its healing odours.

"Thank you, Jack. You must leave us alone now until morning."

He turned to leave but was stopped.

"There is one more thing I need you to do."

She handed Jack the key to Max's motel room.

"I can't explain why but I have a feeling it is important you go there."

In the motel parking lot, the late model green sedan and its occupant sat quietly with the lights off. The mild-mannered man was waiting for the RCMP Bronco to leave. He reached under the front seat and brought out a small, black case with a chrome clasp on either side of the handle. He snapped it open to reveal a pistol, a silencer and six bullets, each nestled in fitted gray Styrofoam. In the lid of the case, and held by an elastic strap, was a pair of black cotton gloves, which he put on. With his eyes fixed on the Bronco he released the clip from the handle and fed the six bullets into it with practised touch, then slapped it back into place with the butt of his hand. The same hand released the silencer from the case. He stopped midmotion. The two officers were getting into their Bronco. For what felt like an hour to the occupant of the green sedan, the Bronco remained in place.

It was, in fact, three minutes. The length of time it took the Bronco to radio to dispatch to tell them Unit 403 was back on the road.

CHAPTER 26

ULYSSES IS RESCUED

JACK WAS DEFINITELY PUSHING THE SPEED LIMIT IN HIS MID-BLUE 2010 Subaru Outlander with all-wheel drive and manual transmission. But he reasoned that everyone at the small local RCMP detachment was home in bed. All four of them, given the hour. He bought the car last year in Edmonton and paid just under $6,000. The fact there is no sales tax in Alberta made the whole deal possible. The asking price had tapped him out. The Harman Kardon sound system interfaced nicely with the playlists on his iPhone, and the 71 cubic feet of cargo space could handle six hockey bags as long as one of them didn't belong to a goalie. The motel sign was the only lonely light on the distant horizon, and it came up quickly to meet him. Jack pulled into the parking area and saw they had six guests that night. There was a dark green sedan parked in the corner, but his attention was drawn to the big black pickup backed into 107.

"That's weird. Why's it backwards?" he wondered aloud.

As Unit 108 was unoccupied he pulled into there and got out. He approached 107 and stopped in his tracks. Something was wrong. The wood around the door lock was splintered. It had been jimmied. Instinctively Jack checked the taser on his belt and felt comfort in its presence. Silently and slowly, he pushed open the door, his eyes adjusting to the darkness. There was a shape in the bed on the far side of the room. He took a step into the room and felt the sound of metal against his skull from the inside of it.

"What the fuck??!!" as he stumbled to the ground.

As his head cleared, the next thing he heard was the sound of a hand weapon being cocked.

"Whoa man. Chill for chrissake. That hurt! Take what you want, I don't give a shit. I don't live here!"

Jack struggled to his feet to face a man shorter by eight inches and lighter than himself by 100 pounds. Under other circumstances you might say he had a pleasant face on a small head on which most of the hair was gone. But his eyes were hard as granite and he had the gun. And the gun had a silencer on it.

"Why don't you just take what you want, and we'll all go home, OK? What are you looking for?"

"Found it," the man said with a voice so cold it sounded like it came from a deep freeze. He cocked his head toward the bed. Jack rubbed the bump on his head, scratched his belly then saw the sleeping dog.

"You came to steal a dog? So, take him. I don't care. How come he's sleeping?"

The man pulled back the bedspread.

"Oh shit. Looks like he's been shot."

"You're a quick study, aren't you kid?"

Jack was getting nervous, pulling at his shirt and his belt.

"No kid. I don't steal for a living."

"Hold it, dude. You're going to kill a… a dog. A wounded dog?! I don't fucking believe you!"

"Believe me."

With his eyes locked on Jack, the man approached the side of the bed. He slowly raised the gun. In the instant he flicked his eyes over to the dog to be sure of his target, Jack unholstered his taser and fired. The twin barbed electrodes raced toward the man and implanted themselves into his neck. At that exact instant the electrical circuit was completed and a charge of 50,000 volts pulsed into the man's body. It went rigid and the man fell to the side on his face. As he hit the floor there was a muffled *'thrump.'* The gun had discharged. The convulsed muscles in his hand had pulled the trigger. The bullet entered under the man's chin, went through his mouth and exited out of the top of his head, lodging in the cheap wood veneer paneling a foot above the floor. Jack screamed in shock and fell to his knees, holding his head in his hands. He stayed like that for several minutes, panting, gulping, gasping, until the initial shock wore off. Breathless and very frightened, Jack pulled himself together. He tried not to look at the dead man but couldn't help it. He knew for sure the next bullet would have been for him. He got up slowly and took a deep breath. Then another. He collected the wires from his taser and stuffed them into his pocket. Then he went to the door and peered out, but everything was normal. Quiet and normal. One o'clock in the morning quiet and normal. *Besides,* Jack reasoned, *there wasn't much noise really. A lot of violence but not so much noise that anyone would notice.* Jack walked over for a closer look at the dog. *My God, he's big! And my God he's beautiful.* At that moment, he remembered Soleil's last words:

"I can't explain why but I have a feeling it is important you go there."

Did she mean the dog? How could she know there was a dog here? That's crazy. That just doesn't make sense.

Jack did a quick look around the room in search of another explanation. All he could find was a man's overnight bag. *The guy in the pickup,*

I guess. And a small black case with, what on quick examination, looked like some drug paraphernalia. *A druggie, maybe? The Healer wouldn't send me all this way for that.* Jack sat down on the side of the bed, rubbed his head, and looked at the white dog sleeping deeply, the red fur around his wound rising and falling rhythmically. *Damn he's big and damn he's beautiful. And there's something, dunno, strange about him. Can't explain it.* With the adrenalin rush wearing off, Jack began to feel tired. He thought hard for the next five minutes and came to the conclusion that it had to be the dog Soleil had sent him here for, and that he should get the animal to her somehow. And, of course, he had to report the dead body. That could wait. No need to wake up the Mounties. But he should report it before the housekeeping staff came in. It would look really bad for him if he didn't. Maybe they had security cameras. Maybe cost him his job at the university, and he sure didn't want that to happen. So, Jack turned his 2010 Subaru Outlander around and backed it as close to the door of Unit 107 as he could, next to the black pickup. He opened the hatchback and smoothed out the moving blanket he used as a floor cover. Back in the motel room, he picked up Ulysses. Although Jack weighed in at 240 and was in pretty good shape, he strained to lift the dead weight of a dog nearly half his body weight. Struggling, he placed the still-sleeping animal in the back of the Outlander. With one last quick look inside the room, he pulled the broken door as closed as it would go, got into his car and drove back onto the highway in the direction of Athabasca University.

He wanted to call the Healer but he didn't have her number. But no matter, they would be there soon. His mind returned to the dead man and he knew he had to phone in a report. He really didn't want to be identified or implicated because of what happened two years ago. So, at 100kmph at 1:23 in the morning, Jack dialled 911. He had no idea where the operator was located. Edmonton? Athabasca? Didn't matter.

"This is 911. What is your emergency?"

Jack took a deep breath and spoke as quickly as he could.

"Room 107 Blue Cedars Motel on highway 2 there's a dead man there and it might be suicide maybe drugs too. Bye now." Click.

Jack reasoned that because of the brevity of the message it would be difficult if not impossible to trace.

Bye now? BYE NOW?! Did I actually say, bye now? What a dork!

Well, he reasoned, he had at least done his civic duty and, with any luck, anonymously. He would go back to the motel in the morning and see what was going on but in the meantime, he had to deliver the dog to the Healer. But she had said she didn't want to be disturbed until morning, so his only option was to take the dog home, where he lived with his mother. He followed Highway 2 into Athabasca until it made the 90-degree left turn and ran out of town to the west. Four miles later it swung north, and he passed a sign declaring that Gull Lake was 12 miles further along. He found the gravel road from the highway and followed it the short distance to the lake. His headlights illuminated the road that Jack could have driven blindfolded. He pulled in beside his family's modest house and killed the engine. He had to clear a place to put the dog and do it very quietly. In the last couple of years, his mother had had to deal with him coming home in the middle of the night, but this was different. He wasn't drunk or accompanied by an RCMP constable. This was definitely different. Silently, he clicked the door open and the floor creaked almost imperceptibly under his size 14 shoe. In a flash, the lights were on and he was face-to-face with his mother wearing a flowered nightgown and a 12-gauge shotgun.

"Aw Momma-Ene, it's only me. I'm really sorry, I tried to be quiet."

"You sneeze a mile from here, son and I'll hear ya."

"Yeah, Momma-Ene, I know."

The woman returned the shotgun to it cradle on the wall above her bed and turned to face her son.

"Momma-Ene, there's this thing, see…"

"What have you done this time?"

"It's nothing like that. Well, maybe it is… There's this dog, see."

His mother fixed him with the kind of gaze she reserved for special occasions. Jack felt like he was 10 again and 4 foot 6 inches tall.

"Dog?"

She made the word sound three syllables long.

"It's a long story, Momma-Ene, but I've got this wounded dog in the car. I think he was shot and somebody tended the wound. Can I tell you the story in the morning?"

No way his mother was going to wait until the morning. Not a chance.

"So, where's you get him? Does his owner know you have him?"

"No, no Momma-Ene, it's nothing like that. I didn't steal him. Honest. I gotta bring him in."

Jack's mother didn't move a muscle. It was as if she had been transformed to stone on the spot. Finally, she spoke. Quiet and level.

"There's no way a strange dog, hurt or not, is coming inside this house."

"But Momma-Ene, he's hurt and unconscious. He's not going to hurt anyone, I promise."

"Put him in the shed. His fleas and vermin will be happy there. The *shed*, son!"

Jack knew it was useless. His mother had made up her mind. The rain would stop raining and the snow would stop snowing if she made up her mind to it. He went outside to the 10-by-10 shed, and by moving some tools around and pushing the snowblower back into the corner, he made enough room for a sleeping pad for the dog. When he opened the trunk door, he saw that the dog had started to wake up, his eyes blinking heavily. He tried to raise his head, but it was too heavy, and it flopped back on to the furniture blanket. His mouth made a dry squishy sound and he was panting lightly. Jack pulled the furniture blanket until the dog was almost at the bumper. Then he put his arms under the blanket and lifted it and its heavy cargo out of the car as one. With his feet unsure on the dark gravel roadway, he struggled to move the dog to the shed. Once there he fell heavily to his knees then placed the dog and the blanket onto the earthen floor as gently as he could. He found a large yellow plastic bowl hanging on the wall and filled it with water from the hose outside. After placing the bowl close to the animal, he stood and left the shed. Jack decided to leave the door slightly ajar to let the fresh night air fill the stuffy cabin. He returned to the house and was relieved to see that his mother had returned to bed. He leaned over to kiss her cheek then turned off the tiny nightlight on the way to his room. Jack had to admit to himself that he couldn't remember ever being so totally exhausted. It had been one helluva 24 hours – especially the last 12. He kicked off his shoes but that was as far as he got. As he flopped on the bed, feet hanging over the end, images of his recent experiences began to flicker in his mind's eye. But with two deep breaths, Jack Mercredi, 22 years of age and a full-blooded member of the Dene Nation, was asleep. And he slept the sleep of the gods.

CHAPTER 27

MAX PFISTER FINDS A BENEFACTOR

MAX AWOKE SLOWLY, STRUGGLING TO GET HIS BEARINGS. THE FIRST thing he noticed was how normal he felt. A little weak and thirsty, but surprisingly well. The second thing he noticed was the powerful, acrid smell in the air. It was on his clothes, it was on him, it was everywhere. He tried to place the smell. Burnt wood or bark for sure. Maybe cedar. Something sweet and flower-like. And another slightly metallic scent he couldn't identify. He rubbed his eye with a knuckle from his left hand and scanned the room. The third thing he noticed was the woman lying on the floor. She was dressed in a long floor-length printed dress and looked like she was sleeping; there was a soft knitted bag beneath her head. He gazed at her. There was something faintly familiar. Slowly and a little shakily he swung his legs off the bed and stood up. To his surprise, he found his balance and felt strong. He knelt beside the woman and discovered she was drenched in sweat. The dress clung to her full figure and her hair was matted. Max shook her gently.

"Lady, are you all right? Miss? Hello?"

Soleil stirred, and startled, sat bolt upright. She shook her head and saw Max looking at her with a mixture of curiosity and concern.

"Why, yes. Yes, I am … I am fine, thank you.

She struggled to get up and Max helped her into the only chair in the room. An involuntary shiver ran through her body, so Max pulled the blanket from the bed and wrapped it around her damp shoulders. Then he sat down on the bed. Soleil took a moment to compose herself then looked carefully at her patient. She took his head in her hands and looked deeply into his eye.

"Your eye is clear, your breathing is regular and your skin is not clammy. How are you feeling?"

As Max returned her gaze, a glimmer of recognition came to him.

"Ahh, I think I feel… fine, thank you. OK. Thirsty, perhaps a little hungry, but my equilibrium is good, and my vision is clear."

"That's good to hear. You were very sick when they brought you in last night. Very sick."

"I don't remember anything except being in the diner and passing out."

He strained his memory for clues of the event and found one.

'Poison," he said softly. "I was poisoned."

"Yes, you were," the Healer replied, equally softly.

The two participants in the recent life-and-death battle sat quietly, each absorbed in their own thoughts. Max looked into Soleil's gentle, kind face.

"You saved me, didn't you."

It was a statement not a question. Soleil looked at him steadily, wordlessly.

"How did you do it? Did you know what the poison was? How did you find an antidote here in the middle of nowhere? This all seems impossible!"

Soleil ran her fingers through her hair to fluff it up and help it dry.

"There are many answers to your questions, but they are unimportant. What is important is that you are well and unharmed."

"But you must tell me what you did. I have trained in the medical sciences and I understand these things."

"You have trained in white man's medicine and there are many things that white man's medicine does not understand. And that you do not understand."

"But your treatment. Did the burning have something to do with it?"

He sniffed at his sleeve.

"It's still there. I can still smell it. What was it?"

"You are better, and the fates have played a part. It was not your time."

Max realized he wasn't going to get what he was looking for. He sat quietly on the bed looking at the woman in front of him. His shoulders relaxed and his voice became softer.

"We have met before, haven't we?"

Again, a statement not a question. Soleil nodded.

"Yes, twice. And possibly a third time."

Max shifted uneasily and stared at a faraway spot on the floor.

"You don't like me because you think I was harsh with your husband when I came to buy that dog."

Soleil forced him to meet her gaze.

"You were unkind to him and you wanted to take something very special and important to us and to our daughter. It is not important whether I like you or not. That dog was a part of our family. I nursed him with my own milk for six months. He is…was, our spirit guide."

"You hated me yet you…"

"I have no hate in my heart for you. Pity perhaps, but no hate."

Though he couldn't show it, Max was deeply moved. Then his mind returned to Ulysses. He stood up quickly.

"Where are we? Where am I? What is this place?"

Soleil explained everything to Max, who was getting more agitated by the minute.

"I have to get back to the motel! I have some important… things there! Where do I find a taxi?"

"There are no taxis here at the university but perhaps I can find someone who will drive you. The motel is not far away. Fifteen minutes perhaps."

"Yes, do that. And be quick about it!"

CHAPTER 28

ULYSSES NEEDS TIME TO HEAL

THE HALF-LIGHT OF DAWN BEGRUDGINGLY REVEALED A SMALL COMmunity of 12 houses forming a shallow horseshoe along the west shore of Gull Lake. In a short time, the sun would pierce the trees opposite and each of the houses would burst into light and welcome another day. Several of the buildings had a dock with a boat or two tied to it. There were whitefish and lake trout in these waters, and they afforded the enterprising residents a modicum of a living. The lake was like glass on this morning with the shoreline pines and cedars being perfectly reflected in the dark water. It was a scene of peace and tranquility.

Perhaps it was the birdsong that awakened Ulysses; perhaps it was the complete stillness of the trees. It was as if he had been awakened by both sound and silence at the same time. He raised his head and scented, picking up little more than the bucolic smell of the forest and the nearby lake. He stirred and a streak of pain shot through his shoulder, a reminder he had been hurt by the humans. He lay back down and slowly began to feel each of his extremities. His hind legs responded to his mental command to move. His tail too. He had been sleeping on his left side all night and it was a little stiff, but nothing more. Ulysses knew the hurt was in his right shoulder and the feeling it made when he tried to put weight on it was very bad. He had never had pain like this in his life. He knew he was hurt, and he knew what he had to do. He had to follow the centuries-old instinct formed in another age. An age before humans lived here and the land was very different. An instinct passed along to him by every forebear whose traces he carried in his body to this day. He must find a warm, dark, quiet and solitary place in which to heal. He would stay there until he was strong again or until he died. Whichever came first. He would deal with the ache in his heart for his family later.

With a great effort Ulysses managed to stand and, despite the initial flash of pain, he knew he could walk. Not fast, but fast enough. His first shaky steps led him to the yellow water bowl, and he drank every drop then limped through the open door of the cabin. On the gravel road his intuition told him to walk away from the lake and away from its people. Soon he found himself at a long black highway, which he crossed and half-slid down the embankment on the opposite side. There was a small creek running parallel to the highway and Ulysses followed it. A massive boulder forced it to turn to the right and it babbled off into the woods. Ulysses stopped and drank again then resumed the trail the little river had forged. Slowly but surely the river grew in width, depth and tempo as it swirled and gurgled on its journey. From the shore, Ulysses saw a big brown trout tantalizingly still just beneath the surface. He stood absolutely still and watched the fish remain in place against the current, his tail undulating slowly from side-to-side. Suddenly Ulysses pounced onto the water, jaws open, forelegs outstretched. The fish was too quick for him and all he ended up with was a mouthful of water and a painful reminder of his injury. Back on the shore he shook himself dry. Turning his head as far as he could, he could just see the wound with his right eye. He reached for it with his tongue to comfort the pain. It helped but not much. He surveyed the forest around him and his eyes fell on the root ball of a big, old spruce tree that had lost the battle with the last big wind that went through. He limped over to it and saw that it made an almost perfect small cave. His nose told him it was recently formed and no other animal he been here. Ulysses stepped down into the earthy indentation and turned in a circle four or five times to tamp down the damp, rough earth. The cave was deep enough that he could curl up in it and not be seen. Which was exactly what he did. Now he needed to sleep and to heal, however long that took. It would take time for his body to mend the damage inflicted on it by the humans. As he rested his head between his paws, he remembered the bad man in the black coat. The bad man who had cracked him on nose with his special stick until he tasted blood. The bad man who had chained him in the back of his truck for such a long time. The bad man who he had escaped from. But the bad man had found him again somehow and was kind to him. Warm and gentle. How had the man found him? And how did he save him from the humans who had hurt him? With images of the past two days swirling in his memory, Ulysses could hold his eyes open no longer. And he fell into a deep, healing sleep where he would remain for the next four days.

CHAPTER 29

MAX MEETS AN UNWILLING ALLY

THE TELEPHONE IN JACK'S LIVING ROOM AWOKE HIM. IT WAS THE Healer at the university asking if he could drive someone to the Blue Cedar Motel. The passenger would pay $25. Jack agreed and said he would leave right away and be there in fifteen minutes. But Jack wanted to check on the dog first. It would only take a minute. The shed was empty, all the water had been drunk, and the door was swung wide. Jack was completely baffled because the dog was semiconscious when he left him last night and was obviously badly hurt. There was no way he could have just walked away. Was there? But no matter, he had a taxi run to do and the twenty-five bucks would take care of his gas for most of the week.

Twenty minutes later he arrived at the university and saw the Healer standing beside a tall man wearing a blue shirt, well-cut slacks, nice shoes and an eye patch. His hair was slightly disheveled, and he had a very stern face. Not a friendly guy, Jack surmised. Without a greeting to Jack or an acknowledgement to Soleil, he got into the passenger's seat of the Subaru and buckled up impatiently. Soleil called Jack over and spoke in a hushed tone.

"Jack, did you find anything when you got to the motel last night?"

"Well, ma'am. It's a huge story but if it's the dog you are asking…"

"The dog? There was a dog there?"

"The biggest most beautiful white dog I've ever seen. But he was hurt. Shot, I think."

"Shot?" Soleil could not believe her ears.

The car horn blared.

"Kid! We gotta get going! C'mon!"

"Well, I didn't know what to do so I took him home."

"Where is he now?"

"Well I don't actually know because this morning he was not where I left him. I think he wandered off."

The car horn sounded again, a constant annoying blast.

"Kid, get your ass over here and drive this car or I will!"

Soleil handed him a card.

"My phone number in Yellowknife. Call me, please."

I will, ma'am. I will. Gotta go. Bye now!"

Soleil watched as the Outlander sped away. She was deeply concerned about Ulysses. She couldn't explain it even to herself but last night she had such a strong feeling that Ulysses was close by, that something was wrong with him, and the motel had something to do with it. But most important, Ulysses was alive! It had been six months since he disappeared and much of that time Dan had been in a deep depression, though he tried to hide it. Her heart was broken too, especially when she had to try to explain to Akkisuktok what had happened to her spirit friend. No one knew whether he was alive or dead. But something last night had reached out to Soleil. She didn't know what and she didn't know who. But it was one of the strongest psychic messages she had ever received. Ulysses was alive! The thought screamed again in her head and in her heart. Reaching for the hem of her long-flowered dress, she sobbed tears of joy into it. Soleil buried her face in the soft cotton that still smelled of last night's cleansing and wept till she could weep no more. Ulysses was alive! Dan and Akkis would be overjoyed. But where was their beloved animal? Can it survive in the wild after being shot? Soleil got her emotions under control. On the way to the airport she would call Dan and share the wonderful, though confusing, news.

An icy silence filled the Outlander as the two men drove in the early morning sunshine. Jack snuck a glance over at the half-blind man with the hawkish nose who stared straight ahead through the windshield.

"Shouldn't take us too long," Jack said cheerily.

"Just drive, will you? And forget the chatter. All I am interested in is getting there, not your conversation."

Fifteen minutes later, the familiar motel sign was visible down the road, its lights still on even though it was 9:00 o'clock in the morning. As they approached, the man with the eye patch sat upright, straining against his seatbelt, looking at the parking lot they were about to turn into.

"Jesus would you look at that!" exclaimed Jack as he slowed the car to a crawl.

His passenger unsnapped his belt, his hand on the door handle. There were two RCMP Broncos and an unmarked sedan with lights flashing in front of Room 107, boxing in the black pickup. The entire area was circled with yellow tape. There were a dozen people, uniformed and not, some with silver cases, one with a camera. A strobe light flashing inside the room lit up the broken door, adding to the surreal scene. Max could wait no longer. He bolted from the car and ran to the door of 107. A very large Mountie stopped him in his tracks.

"Whoa. Hold it. This is a crime scene."

"But I gotta get in. My dog's in there!"

"What's your name, sir, and what is your business here?"

"Max Pfister, and this is my room and I want my dog."

Jack had gotten out of his car and was standing to the side listening to the conversation, trying to stay as unobtrusive as possible.

"There's no dog in there, sir, and I can't let you in. This is a crime scene. We have to wait for the coroner from Edmonton. Three to four hours, I reckon."

Max looked at the shattered door frame. It was fine when he left the room to go to the diner. He looked at his truck, which appeared undamaged. What had happened? And more important, where was the dog?

"Can I at least get my hat and coat from behind the door?"

"Like I said, sir, this is a crime scene. Talk to the coroner."

"This is my truck. I need to get my iPad out of the glove box."

"Sir, what part of 'this is a crime scene' do you not understand? Now step aside. Please."

Max realized anything further at this time was fruitless. *Damn civil servants! Damn stupid cops. Can't they think for themselves? I just want my goddamn hat and coat!*

Jack watched this exchange and walked slowly back to his car. He could be in deep, deep shit here if he wasn't careful. He was interested that the man had some connection to the dog.

"So, ah... was this dog like, your pet?"

Max spun around ready to put this young Native boy in his place, but he relaxed, and took a deep breath.

"Not my pet. Some local idiots shot him, and I brought him here to see if I could do something."

"So, you dressed the wound?"

Max froze, then slowly turned to the young man, his face inches away.

"How did you know the wound was dressed?"

He leaned in even closer, faces almost touching. His voice went icy quiet.

"Have you been here before?" he hissed.

Jack realized he was perilously close to being in deadly trouble. Not only with the Mounties but with this guy, too. And something told him he'd be better off being in trouble with the cops.

"No, no! I mean, did you help him? Did you, like, I mean, clean the wound? Did you put tape on it? Stuff like that."

Max stared at him. Was this kid for real?

"Just trying to make conversation, mister. That's all."

"Well, don't. Just be quiet. I need to think."

"Hey, no problem, no problem. I'll leave you alone, sure." He paused. "Oh, by the way, any chance I could get my twenty-five bucks?"

Max glared at him. Pulled two bills from his pocket, dropped them at Jack's feet and stormed off in the direction of the restaurant.

"What a jerk." Jack said to himself. "But he gave me thirty bucks. Bonus!"

The money went into his pocket; the Healer's card stayed in his hand.

Ironically, Max found himself at the same table in the restaurant he had occupied the night before. The server, however, was different. A young woman, not unattractive, but thin. *Anorexic thin*, thought Max. *This is a troubled person.*

"Can I get you something, sir?

'Whole wheat toast with butter and jam on the side, and tea, bag on the side."

Max had no choice but to wait for the coroner. Maybe he would have some answers.

CHAPTER 30

TAKING STOCK

MAX WATCHED FROM THE RESTAURANT AS THE BLACK SUV PULLED into the parking lot followed by an ambulance. They joined the RCMP Broncos still in place behind the yellow tape. *'Office of the Coroner'* and a crest were emblazoned on the door in white letters. The ambulance took a position close by, its flashing lights adding to the visual chorus. A plain-looking middle-aged man carrying a small silver case disappeared into the room. Max took him to be the coroner. He walked like he was perpetually tired, or had hemorrhoids, or both. It was just after noon, and Max had been confined to the restaurant all morning. Despite having the biography of DaVinci with him, he was in a foul mood. His room and his truck were still guarded by the tired Mountie, well past his weekly quota of caffeine. Several strobe flashes later, the man left the room and headed in the direction of the restaurant. Two first responders came out of Room 107, wheeling a gurney carrying a shrouded figure. Max, together with most of the people eating lunch, watched as the gurney was expertly collapsed and the body slid into the ambulance. The doors were slammed shut and the ambulance pulled away, lights off, siren mute. There was no rush. The coroner entered the restaurant and was directed to a table across from Max, who closed his book and looked up.

"Can I go into my room now? Can you tell that gorilla at the door it's OK?"

"107 is your room? What went on in there? No ID of any kind on the victim. Not even labels in his clothes. Strange. Got any ideas?"

"Not really. I left around 9:30 last night, I think, and everything was normal. Ah… mmm… I returned this morning to this mess and inconvenience."

"You a doctor? Those your instruments? Hypodermic?"

"Vet, actually. Here."

And Doctor Max Pfister presented the coroner with his almost authentic credentials. The man looked at them and, seemingly satisfied, gave them back.

"So, what were you doing with the pillowcase? And the blood-soaked gauze?"

Max's blood turned cold. He had to think fast.

"Well, there was another guest here last night. I met her in the restaurant. Edith somebody. She had come down from Slave Lake with her latest rescue cat and was laying over on her way to Edmonton where she was going to be spayed. The cat, not Edith."

The coroner didn't smile.

"Well, we got to talking and I told her I was a vet and I would do it for her for $50 right here and now and she wouldn't have to drive all the way into the city and pay city prices. Well, she thought that was a grand idea and she agreed. I offered to let her watch, but she said no."

The coroner looked at him. Max had no idea if he was buying the story.

"So, the surgery was completed in half an hour – at the cost of one pillowcase. I guess I'll have to square that with the management. She collected her sleeping cat in its cage and left last night sometime after I left. Or maybe before I got back this morning. One or the other."

Max laughed a hollow laugh. Mercifully, they were interrupted by the coroner's female assistant, who reported that the crime scene had been fully processed and suggested they should probably be getting back. After all, they had a customer waiting. The coroner smiled. Max forced another hollow laugh. A little black humor among colleagues, as it were. The coroner and his assistant left; Max had no desire to stay there a moment longer. There was still much to be done and still many unanswered questions, like where the hell was the dog? It was injured. It was drugged. He couldn't have left by himself. Conclusion: someone had stolen Ulysses. Someone has the dog. But who? Where? And the dog should have further medical attention. Max's thoughts shifted to the events of last night; someone poisoned him, of that he was certain. It was not a random act and it would have been orchestrated by only one person. There was no other explanation. Max had dipped his toe into the world of international intrigue and big money and had come close to having his leg bitten off. A thought struck him, and he reached for his phone. He connected to a particular link and waited.

"You miserable son-of-a-bitch!" he said aloud.

The woman at the adjacent table looked up from her salad. Max's bank account showed a credit of $100,000 followed by a debit of the same amount five days later. Max expected that. But what he did not expect was that what was left of the original $100,000 payment had been drained from his account, also leaving a balance of $1. *How the hell can he do that?!* Max was furious. *That's impossible to do unless… unless…you own the bank!*

"SHIT!" he again said aloud.

He threw a $10 bill on the table, slammed his book shut, and stormed out into the parking lot. He retrieved his hat and coat, his garment bag and his instruments, and soon found himself traveling north at slightly over the speed limit. He wasn't quite sure why he was going north, but it felt right. Somehow, eventually, the dog would resume its journey north, he reasoned. Max concluded that as there were no choices of roads to follow in this barren part of the world, his best chance of finding Ulysses was to travel on the main northbound highway.

Max was also dealing with the feeling that something in him was changing, shifting. The long empty highway afforded him time to think. And the first thought to enter his mind was that he had come close to death last night, and someone saved his life. McCord's wife, Max knew, detested him, but had actually kept him alive – somehow. Some sort of Native cure? Hocus pocus? He had a distant memory of an incantation or a chant. Something. Whatever it was, it worked, and with no apparent after-effects. Max found himself tormented by the knowledge that someone who hated him would have saved his life. It wasn't supposed to work that way. Not in his world. Not in his father's world. Would he have done the same thing if the situation were reversed? Hell no, especially if he hated the person. Let them die. It's probably their fault anyway. I have the power over you, and I choose not to help you. I am the powerful. I am the survivor. I am the winner!

But Max didn't feel much like a winner right now. As the road skirted Athabasca, Max felt as empty as the vast and desolate wilderness displayed before him as if projected onto the windscreen of his truck. His pain and confusion were eating at the edges of his being, and for the first time in his life he felt a change happening within him. He couldn't understand it. There were questions nibbling at the edges of his psyche like termites on the foundation of a poorly built house. And also, for the first time in his life, Max was frightened. Frightened right to his core.

CHAPTER 31

ULYSSES MEETS AN ADVERSARY

IT WAS THE SOUND OF A DISTANT HOWL THAT AROUSED ULYSSES from his long, healing hibernation. It was powerful and primal. It filled his cave and invaded the surrounding forest. Stiffly, Ulysses emerged from his lair and stretched this way and that, arching his back and reaching as far as he could with his forelegs, then his hindlegs. More thirsty than hungry, he returned to the stream nearby and drank to his stomach's content. Sated, he scented again and found the direction from which the sound was coming. He walked past his cave and deeper into the woods, eyes scanning the dark forest. His shoulder no longer caused him pain and he felt strong. Then, not far away, he saw them. Five wolves at their lair. Four were lying down while the alpha male stood guard, vigilant, possessive, scenting the air. He stood perfectly still when he picked up Ulysses's scent, and his pale brown eyes fixed on him. Ulysses walked slowly toward him, fully aware of what was about to happen. There was no turning back. He was challenging the alpha male's domination and intruding on his territory. The alpha male was almost black with a few light patches. His fur was full, but he had a wiry, wily way about him. His pale brown eyes were riveted on Ulysses, with killing his only object. The wolf walked slowly toward Ulysses, his head low, his hackles up, ears flat. His eyes were wide, and his jaws made a clicking sound. The two animals circled this way then the other, looking for an opening. In a flash, the wolf was upon Ulysses, bowling him over, snarling savagely. Ulysses regained his footing and turned to challenge. Ears back, fangs bared, the two animals circled slowly waiting for the other to show a weakness. The wolf was the smaller of the two combatants and, Ulysses knew, probably quicker. Ulysses had the strength and size; his adversary had the speed and the wild guile. The wolf struck for Ulysses's throat but missed, tearing the bigger animal's lip instead. Ulysses tasted his blood. Generations of domestic breeding fell away and Ulysses knew he had been here before, long, long ago. This was not strange to him. He had fought and killed like this a hundred times in a hundred lives before. He felt the stirring of old and strong instincts long forgotten, imprinted into the hereditary history of his breed. Ulysses circled, ready. As wolves do, the alpha male lunged and retreated, in and out, always circling, mouth slathering, lips curled, fangs clicking and clacking. Suddenly, Ulysses charged, hitting the smaller animal square in the ribs with his shoulder. Winded, the wolf retreated to gather himself. The other animals in the pack stood quietly to the side unmoved by the performance of life-and-death theater playing out before them. The wolf lunged, Ulysses sidestepped, slashing the top of the wolf's head with his teeth. The animal howled as blood flowed into his eyes. In that moment of pause, Ulysses, fighting with intelligence as well as strength, saw an advantage. He lunged in low and clamped his jaws on the wolf's foreleg. The sound of crushing bone was followed by a savage, primal howl of pain that reverberated through the forest. Small birds took wing. Ulysses was tiring and his adversary, even hobbling with a useless dangling foot, was still dangerous. Ulysses feinted to one side and moved lightning fast to the other. He struck at the throat where vulnerable arteries run close to the surface, and his teeth made firm contact with the wolf's flesh. Ulysses held the wolf in a death grip and felt and heard the animal's esophagus and windpipe crush and collapse in his jaws. Then the blood began in great quantity, covering Ulysses's front legs and muzzle. He could taste it. It was different from his own. Ulysses found he was enjoying the killing. It was the strongest animals that survived. The ecstasy of killing was the ecstasy of life, and never was it greater that when death was imminent. The wolf, weakened and voiceless, eyes wide with the terror of his impending death, could do nothing. Still Ulysses held his grip. Mercy was something of another time and another place. Slowly, as his life ebbed into the leaves and twigs of the forest floor, the wolf went limp. A hundred heartbeats later, Ulysses released his grip and let his dead adversary flop to the ground. He raised his head to the sky that looked down on to the treetops, and called up a mighty howl to let the forest and all its inhabitants know that,

He, Ulysses, was alive!

He, Ulysses, was the victor!

He, Ulysses, was the strong one!

An immutable law of nature had prevailed once again.

Ulysses, cut and bloodied and panting, walked slowly toward the pack. They all knew the law of the forest. Ulysses had killed the alpha male. Ulysses is the alpha male. The King is dead. Long live the King. As he approached, the four wolves stood to face him, unsure. Their mixed scents confused Ulysses, but he knew one was in estrus. He sought her out and they touched noses. She was beige with three white feet and dark brown ears. And, as always, those piercing brown wolf eyes. The other female and the two adolescent males quietly separated themselves. Slowly, insistently, Ulysses nudged the female deeper into the woods, and they were soon out of sight of the lair. The three remaining animals, paying no attention to the corpse of their fallen leader nearby, returned to the lair and curled up to sleep. He would be food for them all later.

Wolves are pack animals with strict social systems, but although he was the new alpha, Ulysses stayed for only a few days. He was, after all, not a wolf. His was of a different line of succession. On the second day, Ulysses left the lair to drink in the stream and walked further downstream than he had gone before to where the river widened and deepened and ran faster. As he walked, the surrounding vegetation changed too, with lush forest and tall trees giving way to a harsher environment populated by tough little blueberry bushes and shrubs growing between the rocks. Ulysses found a large boulder warmed by the noon-day sun and climbed on to enjoy its comforting warmth beneath his fur. As he lay there, the yearning began to stir in his soul again, absent for such a long time. His need for his human family was always a part of him, but the rhythm of his life and his quest to return home had been diverted. The killing of the wolf had directed Ulysses to a more primitive place, a more basic survival-driven state of being that had remained with him through the mating and his time with the infanticipating female and her pack. It was not the way of nature that he should stay for the whelping. His long-neglected restlessness returning, he knew that soon he would have to leave this place and resume his greater purpose – to be reunited with his human family. And nothing would stop him. He would leave at the next dawn, and two full moons later, the timeless ritual of birth and renewal of the species would happen.

With her time to whelp approaching, the female began to prepare an area in which to give birth, slightly apart from the others in the lair. Ulysses was now many miles away. She tamped down the earth and brought some leaves onto the cave. For two days she lay in place, waiting. On the morning of the third day her labor began in earnest and she panted heavily. She gave a low growling howl, and the first pup emerged from the birth canal. She greeted it by biting thorough the placenta sack, which she quickly ate before beginning to wash the new arrival. It wiggled and uttered the tiniest sound. Even before that task was completed the next pup arrived and she repeated the sequence of events. And so it was for the next two. The other three adults in her pack sat impassively outside the cave. All they could do was watch. When she bit into the birth sack to release the fifth puppy, the animal was motionless. A small black ball with no life in it. The mother sniffed at it, turned it over with her muzzle, and licked it. Satisfied it was dead, she began to eat it. Nature wastes nothing and nature has no place for feeling or sentimentality. She needed the nourishment provided by the by-products of birth, and a stillborn pup was nothing more than that. The female returned to cleaning the four pups that were gathering around her nipples, their tiny mouths and noses searching for something their imprinting over the generations told them was there. The first two latched on while the other two searched and wriggled and squeaked. The female's panting became slower, but she remained on her left side. With a low growl and a push, the final pup emerged. Her movements were slowing; she was tiring. When she bit through the birth sack, she didn't eat it, and began to wash the last of her litter. One of the adolescent males took a step forward to retrieve the birth sack and was greeted with a vicious snap from the mother, which would have torn his flesh if he hadn't jerked back. His reflexes had saved him from a nasty wound. There is no place for a male when a female is whelping, and any creature who intrudes in that process does so at great pain and peril. The noon sun warmed the five puppies, each of whom was tasting their mother's milk for the first time. Their delicate soft fur was dry, and they wiggled and tumbled over each other. It would be two weeks before their eyes would be ready to see their new world. As dusk approached, the female disengaged from her puppies and stepped outside the birthing area. She licked and cleaned herself and went to the stream for water. The other wolves watched her and gave her a wide berth as she returned. She settled back into her place, and with her muzzle managed to turn each puppy so it was lying in the right direction for its next feeding. While Ulysses had resumed his journey, the cycle of life played out in the forest he had left.

Ulysses would never know that soon after the birth, a hungry Grizzly mother would find the lair, scatter the pack, kill the mother-wolf and devour most of her and her litter. The smaller animals in the woods – the fox and the wolverine – would feed on what was left over. As violent as She often is, Nature always maintains a pure balance. The hungry Grizzly is strengthened to feed her cubs, the well-fed fox is now ready to breed, and the carrion birds will take whatever is left back to their wide-mouthed young in their nests high in the branches of the trees. Nothing in Nature is wasted, and although life often takes a different path and purpose from its original intent, life always continues and thrives.

CHAPTER 32

LUNA SAYS GOOD-BYE

LUNA AND DYLAN STOOD ON OPPOSITE SIDES OF THE HIGHWAY, which stretched for five miles in both directions without a hump or a bump or a curve for as far as the eye could see. Luna had resumed her Lucas wardrobe and persona. They had to deal with the fact that they were going in opposite directions. She north and he south to Edmonton. They stood together in the middle of the highway unsure of quite what to do. Lucas spoke first.

"So, I guess we should say goodbye in case a ride comes along, right?"

"Guesso... So, um... so long, and I really hope you get to Yellowknife, OK. I mean, safely. Oh shit, I mean... that you actually get there! Man, that came out all wrong. I'm really sorry."

"It's OK. I get it. No worries. I'll be fine."

"Just in case you want to, here's my uncle and aunt's email address. But only of you want to, you know..."

"Sorry I can't do the same. I don't actually know if they will be there or anything. I don't know what I will do if I can't find them."

Despite her resolve, a sniffle escaped, and quickly disappeared on her sleeve. Dylan pretended not to notice.

"You can always email me and we could figure something out. I wouldn't mind if we got together again."

"Yeah, me too. I could do that."

"Like I wouldn't mind checking out Yellowknife."

"Yeah...."

And with that, they ran out of conversation. They shuffled their feet, walked a few steps this way and that, and ended up back in the same place. In the distance, in the southbound lane, a large truck came into view. They could hear its gears downshifting. Luna grabbed Dylan around the waist and held him tight.

"Bye, Dylan. I had a great time. You have been really nice to me."

"Easy girl, I haven't gone yet!"

"Yes, you have."

The truck was a large moving van and came to a noisy idle beside the two young people. The driver leaned out his window.

"Come on. In ya get. I can take you as far as Edmonton if that helps."

Dylan ran around to the passenger's door, climbed up on the stainless-steel footstep and swung his backpack in behind the seat. He shut the door. The driver looked at Lucas.

"What about your buddy?"

"Well, she... *he's* heading north – to Yellowknife."

The driver stuck his curly red head out the window.

"That's a helluva journey young fella. I really think you should come along with us. I know it's backtracking but there's a gas station and snack bar, no more than five miles down the road at Enterprise. And it's at a highway junction so you will get more traffic. C'mon, jump in. It's not safe for you here alone. There's wildlife, you know?"

Luna needed no more convincing and took her place beside Dylan. The big van slowly returned to speed, and soon its rear lights were no more than a speck in the distance.

CHAPTER 33

LUNA AND MAX MEET AGAIN

LUNA AND DYLAN SHARED ANOTHER GOODBYE 15 MINUTES LATER, and the moving van resumed its journey to Edmonton with Dylan on board. Luna had about twenty-four dollars left and spent three of it on a Twinkie and a small milk. She asked the man behind the counter if he had a piece of cardboard she could use for a sign. And a marker? He had one in green and Luna started printing her sign in four-inch high letters. She misjudged the length and had no room for the final 'E.' She figured the motorists would get the idea, 'YELLOWKNIF.' As she was shading in the letters, a man entered and approached the counter, credit card in hand. The manager looked up.

"Number 4? Seventy-six dollars, please."

"Could I get a tea with the bag on the side? And an order of whole wheat toast, buttered with jam on the side?"

"Sure. Grab a seat beside the young man there."

Luna glanced up as the man sat down and saw that he was wearing an eye patch. He was also wearing a black, flat-crowned hat and a long dark coat. He looked very scary to her but sat there quietly. He looked out the window and waited for his order, paying no attention to her. His toast and tea finally arrived, and he redirected his attention to them from the empty space he had been occupying. He noticed the sign on the table.

"An almost perfect sign, I'd say," he said with a smile that lacked much warmth.

Luna looked up at him, and once she got used to seeing only one eye, she had to admit it looked like a nice eye. A kindly eye with some smile wrinkles at the corner.

"Yeah, well…"

Max studied the young man's face; there was something familiar about it, but he couldn't quite place it. Never mind.

"Are you really going to Yellowknife? That's a long drive. Family there?"

"Yup." And she returned to her sign.

"Well, I don't know if you are interested, especially because you have already made a sign, but I am going north and maybe even that far. You are welcome to ride with me. You could always keep your sign in case you decide to get out half-way."

The man chuckled and smiled at Luna again. She felt comfortable in his presence, though she noticed that he seemed to be studying her.

"Well, sure. OK. I can't pay you for the gas, but I will look after all my food and stuff."

"That sounds fair. I'll just wash my hands and we'll be on our way. By the way, my name is Max."

"I'm…Lucas. Nice to meet you."

"Same here, Lucas. Excuse me."

By actual count Max and his passenger met only three trucks and five cars coming south in the next five-and-a-half hours. They had been passed by only one vehicle also going north, a motorcycle driving very fast. There was probably no harm in it, Max thought, because the road was flat and straight, and on this day the visibility was unlimited. The driver could see a moose a mile away. Max had gassed up at the truck stop in Enterprise, taken a bio-break, and the girl had bought a snack. Half an hour later they made the turn off from Highway 1, which veered to the west, onto Highway 3, which led straight north. It was the gateway to Yellowknife and the only road to go there.

"What happened to Highway 2?" asked Luna.

"Maybe they're saving it for future development," was all Max could think to say. He set the cruise control to 75mph, safely just over the limit, and relaxed with his thoughts. They talked very little. Max was thankful that his passenger had been quiet most of the journey. It suited him just fine. If there was a single word to describe this part of Planet Earth it would be 'empty.' Mile after mile of two-lane blacktop with a dotted white line down the middle. Max assumed this is what they called tundra; it consisted of broad, low, flat rocks with hardy little bushes growing from the cracks, and the occasional spindly pine. He remembered reading somewhere that these feeble-looking trees were often 50 or 60 years old and had worked hard to grow in this harsh environment, which was frozen solid six months of the year and green for only four. Although the terrain and the season were different, the vastness and emptiness of the land reminded Max of the road he had traveled six months ago with a drugged Ulysses in the back of his truck during the darkest and coldest time of winter. He was forced then, against every instinct, to drive slowly on the snow and ice-covered highway. He remembered that trip vividly, not because of the weather, but because he had made a pact with the devil who had tempted him with a quarter of a million dollars. He didn't realize it at the time, but he had suffered a crisis of conscience. He had agreed to commit a crime, the only criminal thing he had ever done in his life. He had done and said a lot of shitty things to many people, but never deliberately broken the law. And thinking back on it, he hated himself for his weakness. He had always prided himself in being strong and dominant, and certainly he was that academically. In addition, his sled-dog breeding business had started well, and he had the education to make it work. Who else in the north had written a thesis on creating a Super Dog that had been well received by geneticists and scholars around the world? For a short time, at least. He had been very scientific and analytical in his breeding program and in the beginning it worked well. His enterprise in Juneau thrived and he was earning a reputation among professional mushers for producing quality dogs. But then, a perfect storm. Two events occurred concurrently. The first was his plane crash and injury. And the second was that the dogs bred by Dan McCord were doing better in competition than his were. At first, he attributed it to a mathematical anomaly. But after analyzing breeding data from the winning teams from the Iditarod, *The Run,* and the Finnmark in Norway over two years, Max had no choice but to conclude that McCord bred more winners than he did. This was a massive blow to his ego. After all, wasn't he the genius? Didn't he follow the path cut out for him by his father? Etched in his mind was what his father had yelled at him a hundred times, 'You get smart, you get rich, you get popular. Get it kid?' Well he got smart, but his father was wrong on the other two. The man became a fatal accident statistic one drunken night, and Max never got the chance to be angry with him to his face and tell him how wrong he was and what a shitty father he had been. And Max knew he carried that anger and bile in him to this day.

How did McCord do it? He never studied genetics or even went to university as far as Max knew. He seemed to have an instinct when it came to breeding. He seemed to have a connection with his dogs, and everyone knew that a McCord dog would have a good temperament and would work well in harness as part of a team. And McCord's dogs made good team leaders. The very best of them, of course, was Ulysses. Max had little doubt that the McCord-Ulysses team would have won 'The Run' this year. He had to admit he was experiencing a very unfamiliar emotion – envy, mixed with begrudging admiration. McCord was good. His lead dog was exceptional, and he deserved his success. Max tried hard to understand why. WHY had it all happened? What unseen force or influences were at play in McCord's life that were not present in Max's?

On the way to the 60th parallel and the border to the Northwest Territories, they had driven through towns with quaint names like High Level and Meander. But now, on the north side the border, there were no towns. Just empty, tedious highway where the sighting of a crow by the roadside was considered a major event. As the pickup sped through the desolate countryside, Max's thoughts were interrupted by his passenger beside him as he scrunched up the cellophane from the chips bag and put it into the door pocket. He made a pillow from his hoodie and rested his head on the side window, eyes looking outside at nothing in particular, backpack on the floor. Max's mind returned to the conversation he had had with Soleil after he awoke from her treatment for the poisoning that had saved his life. She told him that Ulysses had been fed on her breast milk for the first six months of his life. Did that make for some sort of a… a… spiritual connection? Something unseen and unknown between her and the dog? Is that what McCord had been talking about? Since that day six months ago when the damn dog had escaped from him at the gas station in Jackson, California, Max had been tracing and tracking him, always one step behind as this dog somehow made its way back toward these people whom Max struggled to understand. There was clearly some force at play that was drawing them inexorably together. Max calculated that by this point in the journey, the dog had travelled well over two thousand miles. But HOW?!

It was difficult for Max to see Lucas because the boy was seated on his blind side. He was, however, able to slightly adjust the rearview mirror, which his good eye referenced frequently. *What is it? Why am I so sure I know this boy?* And he cast another glance in his direction. Then it hit him! He knew exactly where he had seen this person before. And this person was a girl. *The* girl. The forest. The red truck. Max was flooded with emotions because he had been gutted ever since he saw that redneck bastard try to rape her – and he did nothing to stop it. Nothing to help her. He let her suffer, and her cries of fear and pain were reverberating in his brain right now. He was so obsessed with the dog that all he cared about was capturing that magnificent white creature. His future depended on it. And it was the dog who had saved her. He was just a bystander. A voyeur, and he hated himself for it.

"Are you all right, Mr. Max?

Without realizing it, he had the steering wheel in a death grip. Every knuckle was white and small beads of perspiration flecked his forehead.

"No, no, I'm fine. Just fine. I just, ah ... I maybe ate my toast too fast. A little indigestion." Max cleared his throat, relaxed his hands and exercised his fingers.

"Yes, yes, I am fine, thank you. So, if you don't mind my asking, who are you visiting in Yellowknife? Do you have family there?"

"I am trying to find my sister. I haven't seen her for a while, and I think she lives there."

Max decided to tread lightly. There was more story here, but he didn't want to seem like he was prying and frighten her off.

"Well, that will be nice for the two of you to get together again."

They drove in silence for a few minutes, Luna lost in her memories of her sister, and Max dealing with his demons.

"So, what's her name?"

"Sorry? Pardon?"

"What's your sister's name?"

"Oh. Her name is Soleil."

For the second time in an hour, Max was struck by an emotional thunderbolt. How could this be possible?! It couldn't be the same Soleil! Could it? Come to think of it, Max vaguely remembered one of the office workers at the clinic talking about The Healer from Yellowknife. Maybe he misheard. Maybe it was delirium. Then again, maybe it was not and this girl, his passenger, was searching for the same Soleil who had saved his life!

The next hour was spent in silence. Max's mind was spinning. There were simply too many interconnected events that had no reason to be connected, but, somehow, were. He did nothing to help the girl who was being attacked. The dog saved her. The dog was shot. Max saved him. Max was poisoned. Soleil saved him. The dog disappeared. Then out of nowhere, by total coincidence, this girl is riding in his truck, and might be the sister of the Healer. He was a man of science and logic. Of action and reaction. Of cause and effect. A believer in the laws of the universe. Of tracking data. Of believing data. Of things making sense. But none of this did. There was a common element among these events but try as he might, he could not put his finger on what it was. The more he thought about it the more he felt that Soleil and the dog were at the epicentre of this bizarre kaleidoscope.

The empty highway ribboned out in front of them and behind, and rarely did they see another vehicle. Another comfortable silence filled the cabin. Max broke it gently.

"How about your folks? Where are they?"

Lucas' mood darkened. He folded his arms across his chest. Max saw the shift in body language in the rearview mirror.

"OK, OK. I don't want to pry. I'm sorry. But let me get this straight. They had two kids, right?"

"I told you that!"

"And their names were…?"

"I told you that too! Soleil and Luna… Oh shit… I mean… Lucas."

Max let a silence play out for as long as it wanted to, then said in a soft voice, "It's OK. I had an idea you were not Lucas, but I didn't want to frighten you. It's a lot more difficult traveling as a girl. I understand that."

"You know, maybe you should let me out. Could you pull over please?"

"I can do that, sure, and you can leave any time you want. But I want you to think about that decision for a moment. It's at least 40 miles to the next town and you've seen how little traffic there is."

Luna chewed at a cuticle on her finger and stared straight ahead at the empty road.

"Here's what I suggest. Let's continue on to the next town. You'll have half an hour to think about what you really want to do. I think that right now you are embarrassed because you had to lie to me to protect yourself. I understand that, and you have no reason to feel bad. Or unsafe. Can you work with that? Miss Luna?"

"I guess…" she said in a little voice.

Max felt that in a curious way he was starting to make amends to this girl. But he still felt like shit in his gut.

"Great," he said and let a silence ride with them for a few minutes.

"Is it OK if I ask you one more question? I'm OK if you prefer to…"

"No, OK. What?"

"What was your mother's name?"

"What? WHY?!"

"Nothing really. I was just curious because she chose two such beautiful and, um… unusual names for you and your sister. I wondered if…"

"Lisa. Her name was Lisa. And my dad was Mike."

"Lisa. That's pretty."

And again, the conversation evaporated as Max returned to his thoughts. 'Lisa' was tantalizingly close to 'Liseli,' which means 'light' in Chippewa. His heart skipped a beat.

CHAPTER 34

ULYSSES JOINS LUNA AND MAX

"MR. MAX! LOOK! STOP! STOP!"

Max could not believe his eyes. Five hundred yards off the highway on top of a rock promontory was Ulysses! Before the pickup stopped, Luna had jumped out and was running toward the dog screaming, *"Hey! Hey Pal!"* In reply, Ulysses raised his nose to the cloudless sky and howled a howl that would make a marble statue smile. He ran toward the girl, and Max lost sight of them behind a bush as they fell to the ground, tumbling and rolling, laughing and slathering. When they reappeared, they were both covered in twigs and leaves. Ulysses stopped and gave himself a shake, which started at his nose, rippled through his body and left through the end of his tail. Luna brushed herself off mindlessly. Ulysses walked close to the girl, who had a handful of the fur of his shoulder. Max clicked on the flashers and got out of the truck. He walked around to the passenger side. Ulysses stopped dead in his tracks. His ears flattened. His eyes widened. The fur on his back stood straight, and he showed his teeth with a low menacing growl that came from a place a thousand years old. Everything said, *Stay away. Do not approach. Danger.* Max stood very still. Luna, however, knew none of the history these two shared.

"Hey pal! It's OK. Stop it. That's Mr. Max and he's OK."

Max took a small step forward and Ulysses's growl became even more menacing. Luna watched, confused and frightened. They were only a few feet apart when Max knelt down and held out his hand. Luna heard him speak in a strange voice. It was musical. It was soothing.

"Hello, my beautiful boy. My very beautiful boy."

Luna watched as Ulysses's body language slowly changed, and he relaxed as Max continued talking to him in that new tone of voice. Luna relaxed her grip on the dog's fur and Max took a slow, short step towards them.

"Can he come with us, Mr. Max? Can he, please?!"

"I have a feeling you'll have to ask him that question. Bring him around the back."

Max unhooked the tailgate and lowered it in invitation. Luna encouraged the dog.

"C'mon boy. Come on. Up you jump. Go on!"

Ulysses's ears stayed back again. The low rumbling growl returned to his throat, and his fangs threatened, white and moist. He backed away from the truck.

"C'mon boy. You can do it? What's the matter?"

Ulysses remained defiant, looking from one person to the other. Wary. Dangerous. The low growl continued to threaten. To warn.

"You know, Luna, maybe he'll go into the back seat. Let's try that. I'm OK with him riding with us if you are…"

"Sure! He's my friend and I love him."

Luna pulled her seat forward and Ulysses, after a brief hesitation, jumped in. They were back on the highway a minute later.

Ulysses found himself beside a flat-brimmed black hat and a folded long coat.

Although Max knew the answer, he thought should ask the question anyway.

"So, how did you and this dog meet?"

The memory was still fresh. Luna took a deep breath.

"Well, I was hitching and had just got off a ride see, and was crossing a stream and I fell in. The dog came outta nowhere and kind of helped me. A little. I woulda been OK you know, but…Well anyways, I went on my way and he did too. Anyways, a little while later like this perv in a red pickup starts to hassle me. I figured I could handle it. I was really scared but I wasn't going to let him know that. He turned out to be a real badass and he grabbed me and like pulled me into the woods. I screamed and kicked but it was just me and him and he was bigger and stronger. He started to pull my sweats down and, and he was touching me like 'down there.'"

Luna's voice broke, and a sniffle smudged her sleeve.

"I was crying and begging him to stop. But he wouldn't. It was really shitty, and I was really scared. Then out of nowhere, my pal came back and WHAM! knocked this asshole off me and snarled at him and drooled spit on him and everything. My buddy here looked like he was about to bite this guy's face off. I pulled myself together. So, do you know what happened next?"

"No, what?" Max asked in a barely audible voice.

"I kicked the son-of-a-bitch right in the balls. Twice! When me and my pal left, he was lying in the mud groaning. Fuckin' A! Anyways, me and the dog hung out. He stayed with me all night, which was a good thing because it was really like spooky in the forest what with all the noises and everything. Then, the next day, I met this really nice guy Dylan, and the three of us hung out camping for a couple of days. Then the dog just took off one night, so me and Dylan continued hitchin' and camping without him. After a while Dylan took off too 'cause he needed to go in the other direction to get to his aunt and uncle's place. Then I met you and here we are."

His heart hollowed out of everything but guilt, Max had nothing to say, but he had to say something.

"That's terrible story and I am so sorry you had to go through it. The dog was obviously looking out for you even though you didn't know it. You are a very fortunate young lady."

"Yeah, I guess I am. I love him even though he took off. That doesn't mean he doesn't love me. He just had to do what he had to do. I think he loves me too. And that makes me happy."

Max was more conflicted than he had ever been in his life. There was no way he could ever tell this girl that he knew Soleil and Dan and their baby. And Ulysses.

"Oh God!" he said under his breath. It was a curse. Not a prayer.

Luna turned around in her seat. She and Ulysses locked eyes and she ruffled the fur around his neck just the way he liked it. She knew he loved her.

CHAPTER 35

MAX AT THE CROSSROAD

MAX FOUND THE ENDLESS MILES OF DRIVING TEDIUM MANAGEABLE because they allowed him to think. He continued to be emotionally confused and intellectually challenged by the number of disconnected events that appeared, in fact, to be connected, but he couldn't understand how and why. *Too many coincidences,* he thought to himself. With the girl half-sleeping, and Ulysses quiet in the back seat, at least he had silence. A conversation he had had with his PhD supervisor and mentor, Dr Arnold Swanson, returned vividly to his mind.

"So, Maximillian, my boy, let us play a little parlor game."

They were finishing a celebratory lunch at the Faculty Club in honor of the completion of Max's PhD thesis, "Super Dog – Genetic Planning to the Perfect Canine." He had completed the two-year program in 14 months, which was, in Max's opinion, two months too long. His impatience always exceeded his academic abilities – which were profound. Swanson began.

"Let's discuss the precept of coincidence. And, indeed, it is a precept, which is defined as, 'A general rule intended to regulate behaviour or thought.' We have all experienced coincidences, have we not? And quite regularly too. Max, describe to me a coincidence in which you have participated recently."

"Well, last month I was in the library looking for Mendel's *Three Laws of Inheritance*. I couldn't remember the third one. I found the book, and next to it, and misfiled, was the next book I was going to look for, Ridley's book on genomes. I think that qualifies as a coincidence, don't you?"

Dr. Swanson sipped his coffee, pausing for effect.

"Absolutely, yes, that is a classic coincidence. But, let me put this to you, Maximillian. What if there were no such thing as 'coincidence?' What if 'coincidence' is nothing more than a way for the powerful to control the masses, not unlike religion. When a grieving mother asks the priest why her baby died, he will say, 'It was God's will.' And that ends the discussion without really answering the question, which is actually a massively complex one. Similarly, you see, saying something is a coincidence is also a convenient way to explain what we cannot explain. Why were those two books adjacent? I invite you to find another answer. But be forewarned, it is challenging, and will take you down many dark intellectual rabbit holes. It will take you to places some call metaphysical, others call spiritual. It will lead you down paths that some label as faith, and others label as love. Journey at your peril, my boy, but I invite you to take the journey."

Max never did take that journey, of course, because at the time he was too busy focusing on the world of science — that which could be quantified and measured — and he had no patience for things metaphysical. Certainly, he had no time to dwell on matters of faith and love. They just didn't have a place in his life. Never had.

Until now. He was searching for an explanation, a reason why all these apparently unrelated people and events were coming together in some way, and he was in the middle of it all with no understanding why. Why had Soleil saved his life? Why had this girl been in the café at the gas station where he just happened to stop? And she was related to Soleil! And they came across Ulysses standing on a rock beside a desolate highway! Why? WHY? As he thought about it all, Max found that his breath quickened, his heart rate increased, and he began to perspire again. He gripped the wheel and his foot pressed down on the accelerator involuntarily. The truck was rocketing down the highway. The girl woke up with a start. She looked at the man. He was rigid. She couldn't see his eye, but his head was locked in place. Perspiration on his forehead and hands. She shook his arm.

"Mr. Max. Mr. Max! What are you doing? Stop it! You are doing 110 miles an hour! Stop! STOP!"

Max was shaken back to reality, but the full-blown panic attack was overwhelming him. He slowed the truck down and managed to turn into a campsite beside a small lake. Even before the vehicle came to a stop, Max jumped out and uttered a scream that shook Luna to her core. He ran toward the lake tearing his shirt off. He kicked his shoes away and pulled off his pants, all the time screaming an inhuman scream. He ran into the water and it wasn't until it was chest-high that he stopped. Suddenly he was immobile and silent. Luna ran to the shore, Ulysses beside her.

"Mr. Max! Come back!"

She waded into the water up to her knees.

"Shit! This is freezing! Mr. Max. Come back! I can't swim!"

She looked at Max 40 feet away and cried out helplessly as she saw him beginning to sink lower and lower into the water. The shock of the ice-cold spring-melt water had paralyzed the man and was sucking the life heat out of him by the second. Luna looked on terrified and helpless as his shoulders disappeared beneath the surface. Ulysses could be a bystander no longer. He jumped into the water and swam strongly toward the man. With no clothing to take in his mouth, he clamped his jaw onto Max's forearm as firmly as he had to but as softly as needed, and began to pull him back to shore. Barely conscious, Max offered no resistance. Once at the little sandy beach, he crawled on his hands and knees back onto the land. He collapsed, weeping quietly. Ulysses shook himself dry and Luna rushed over to Max. Slowly he was able to compose himself as Luna collected his clothes. She ran back to the truck, leaving the man and the dog together. Max wiped the sand from his face and looked at Ulysses, who returned his gaze. There were no words to fill the silence.

"Here, Mr. Max, dry yourself with this. And after you get dressed, you might want to put this on."

And she handed him an adult-sized sweatshirt. She looked bashful.

"Dylan and I traded, you know? Should fit you. You gotta get warm."

It was the heater in the truck that eventually warmed Max. He had been quiet in the hour since they returned to the road, and Luna sat equally quiet, not sure what had happened. Max knew what had happened. His whole world, his entire life had been turned upside down. What was the reason all these things were interconnected? What did all these events share in common?

The answer had come to him.

In a single word.

Love.

CHAPTER 36

ARRIVING HOME

AT MILE 116 ON THE MACKENZIE HIGHWAY IN THE NORTHWEST Territories, just before the turn north onto Highway 3 to Yellowknife, Max came to a conclusion about which he was dead certain. Ulysses had to be returned to McCord and his wife. His decision flew in the face of everything he had learned about how life and success work, everything his father had taught him, everything he knew to be the way of the world. Of his world, at least. Until now. He just had to accept, on the evidence at hand, that a lot of the world worked differently than he did. Many people seemed to have faith and love as the foundation for their lives. He realized he had had some sort of epiphany. And, the dog had saved his life despite everything Max had done to him! Could that be some kind of love too?

Max just knew that reuniting that family was the right thing to do. Throughout his life he had rarely, if ever, 'done the right thing.' He was always too busy being smart or being clever or being hurtful. He was about to make amends. That decision was followed by another, and like the first, Max knew that it, too, was the right thing to do. The only thing to do. But first he had to make amends.

The sky was yellowing as the sun prepared for another night below the horizon, and Yellowknife was less than an hour away. With cruise control taking care of the velocity and his right knee braced against the bottom of the wheel managing the direction, Max brought his tablet to life. He had researched McCord's address when he was making his plans to get Ulysses before the race, and he knew they lived about 12 miles west of Yellowknife. He located the information he was looking for and shut down the tablet. He could avoid going into Yellowknife right now. Their cabin was on the river, which ran south out of Fiddler's Lake, 300 yards from the highway. Max would go into the city after he dropped off the girl and the dog.

About a mile from the Fiddler's Lake Road an unexpected ground fog settled onto the highway, and the further they drove, the thicker it became. Max slowed the vehicle to a crawl.

"Luna, I need you to watch for a mailbox at the end of the lane. Keep your eyes open. It has to be coming up soon."

He was driving at no more than 10 miles an hour with his front wheel on the broken center white line. Even though they hadn't seen another vehicle for nearly an hour, Max clicked on the emergency flashers, and turned the headlight control one more notch to activate the fog lights. The effect was like something out of a space movie. The slow-moving black vehicle looked disconnected from the road with many, many lights trying to pierce the fog, some blinking, some yellow, some white. The mist caused everything to glow in a supernatural way.

"I see it, Mr. Max. I see it. It's right there! I'm so excited!"

Max pulled onto the shoulder and put the truck into park. The box simply said, 'McCord' and had a white painted metal cutout of a dog welded to the top. *It has to be Ulysses,* Max thought.

"Luna, this is where we say goodbye. I will drop you two off here. It's a short walk to the cabin."

"But I'm scared, Mr. Max. Can't you stay with us?"

"You will have the dog with you. He knows where he is going, and he will protect you. Just hang on to him. You'll be fine. Promise."

Max got out of the truck and opened the passenger door for Luna to get out. Then he pulled the seat back forward and Ulysses leapt to the ground. The dog took a moment to get his bearings and scented in every direction. He took a few steps down the gravel roadway, stopped and looked back at the girl and the man. The man was kneeling down in one knee in front of her. He reached out and took her hand. Luna was uncertain but didn't pull away.

"Luna, I need to tell you that I am sorry."

"What for? You have been really nice to me."

"All I can say is that I wasn't always. I know it's confusing for you but please just take my word for it. One day you will understand. I am truly sorry."

Max stood and walked toward the dog. He knelt down again, but this time he was on both knees, as if preparing to pray. Ulysses turned to face him. He scented the man and sensed the same feeling from him as he had the night the man fixed his wounded shoulder. It was like affection, but something more. The man reached out to touch him and instinctively Ulysses pulled back. Then he took a step forward to be closer to the man who gently put his hand on Ulysses's neck and ruffled his fur in that nice way. The two former adversaries locked eyes and stayed perfectly still, as still as the silent, mist-shrouded forest. Max was trying to find words, but they choked in his throat. He struggled.

"Ulysses… Ulysses… I am so, so sorry. For everything. I…"

The sentence hung in the mist as the two remained silently, deeply, connected to each other. Finally, Max cleared his throat and stood. He spoke perhaps a little too brightly.

"Well you two, time to say goodbye. I wish you both happiness at the end of the path. Good luck! Oh, and here's your sweater back."

"No, no, you keep it Mr. Max. Like a souvenir, like?"

"That's very kind of you, Luna, but I won't be needing it anymore. Thanks anyway."

As the truck slowly drove off, Ulysses and Luna were left in the dimness of the late afternoon fog. Although it concealed much of the detail of the path and the forest, it was not dark. Luna couldn't believe her journey was over and she and Soleil would be together again. Her heartbeat quickened. Still, she was in a strange place and afraid of what lurked in the trees. She grabbed a fistful of hair on Ulysses's shoulder, and they walked down the road together. Ulysses scented the dogs some distance off, but they were unusually quiet. He remembered the smell of this forest and its dark carpet of decaying leaves and bark and twigs. How often he had run through it both as a pup and as a grown dog being chased by Akkisuktok, always letting her catch him eventually. His eyes strained to see the cabin as he scented old charcoal in the wood stove. He was getting close and he was getting excited. He quickened his pace and jumped little jumps.

"Whoa, take it easy big fella!"

Luna was barely able to hold on as the dark, squat cabin appeared out of the fog. Ulysses pulled away and bounced toward the door. He barked a greeting, stood up and put his front paws on the door and barked again. He dropped down and looked over his shoulder at Luna who joined him. She knocked on the heavy cedar door, called out, and held her breath.

"Hello? Hello? Anyone home?"

Ulysses jumped up again then fell back down, whining a little whine of excitement. Luna saw the padlock hasp, which had no padlock, but a wooden peg instead. She called out again, then pulled the peg from its place. The door swung open and Ulysses jumped into the dark room.

The cabin was empty.

CHAPTER 37

MAX TAKES A FLIGHT, AND A REUNION

AS MAX STRODE THROUGH YELLOWKNIFE AIRPORT IN HIS FLOOR-length coat and matching black drover's hat, he barely noticed the full-sized stuffed polar bear jumping onto the man-made ice floe in the lobby. As spectacular as it was, his attention was otherwise occupied with searching the signs of the various vendors and concessions. Finally, he saw it, *"Nakla Flight Academy,"* in bright blue letters. And beneath that, *"Charters, Sightseeing, Rentals."* And beneath that, *"Fly the NORTH!"* The concession was staffed by a young man, probably a college student, but more likely a student at the Flight Academy earning some flying hours. Max approached the counter, but the young man's attention was riveted on an article in *Flying* magazine.

"Excuse me!"

'Oh, sorry mister. Fascinating article on microbursts and how they can bring down a 737."

"Really."

"So, what can I do for you, Mr. —?"

"Max Pfister. Doctor Max Pfister. I called ahead."

Max decided that using his full title would help with the fraud he was about to perpetrate. The young man's eyes fell on the papers on the desk. He pulled one out.

"Oh right. You're the pilot from Juneau. You wanted to confirm that your Alaska Pilot's license would be valid here. Well, it is. And you wanted, let me see…Oh yes, a 172 for an hour of touch-and-goes. Right?"

"That's correct. Just want to check out the dusk light. An hour should do it. I'll let the tower know I'm just doing touch-and-goes."

"May I have your license and logbook, please, and a credit card? Oh, and your passport."

Max handed the documents across the counter along with his VISA. This would only work if the young man failed to notice that the expiry date on his pilot's license had been altered. He would notice that Max hadn't flown for five years, but his Pilot's Log was impressive and revealed a pilot with over four thousand hours, most of which were on floats and skis. *He doesn't look like it, but this guy is some bush pilot,* thought the young man.

"So, you want to get back in the air again, is that it?"

Max was beginning to feel fidgety. Not a feeling he liked. He spoke quickly.

"I've been doing a lot of circuit stuff at home recently. Just didn't bother logging it. An hour here, an hour there. Hardly worth the trouble, right?"

The young man continued filling out the paperwork and Max made sure to give him his good profile. He hadn't said anything about the eyepatch and Max wanted to keep it that way.

"Son, any chance you could speed it up a little? Dusk comes and goes pretty quickly, and I want to get as many circuits in as I can."

"Sorry, almost done, sir… Sorry, I mean doctor. You won't have to worry about traffic. The last commercial was an hour ago and the next one isn't until 9:00 p.m. and you'll be back by then, right?"

He pushed the papers toward Max, handed him a pen and indicated where to sign.

"Initial this box if you want the additional insurance."

"I don't think I'll be needing it, thank you."

"Right then. Follow me, Doctor Pfister. The Cessna is on the tarmac just at the end of the building. You've got a little over an hour's fuel. If you want to stay in the circuit for a couple of extra touch and goes, you'll be OK."

"Thank you. I am sure that will be more than enough."

The two men left the building and walked toward the airplane. While the young man untied the wing ropes and removed the chocks, Max did his visual inspection. He had done this a thousand times before but made a point to take his time and appear thorough and experienced.

"I'll spot you until you're clear to the taxiway. The tower is on 102.5, here are the keys, and have a good flight!"

Max got into the four-seater after taking off his hat and coat, which he put on the passenger's seat. He pulled the door shut, clicked the latch and buckled himself in. A feeling of exhilaration was stirring in his belly, and the joy and anticipation of flying came flooding back to him. Despite his five-year absence from this seat, he knew he had forgotten nothing; deep were the imprints on his mind and on his soul. The engine barked to life then settled into a steady thrum as it quickly got to temperature in the warm summer air. Max followed the young man's arm gesture to swing into a right turn and on to the taxiway. He checked in with the tower and was directed to the end of runway. Once there, he swung the little plane around to face down the 7,000 feet of asphalt beckoning to it. Leaning on the brakes, he ran up the engine to check the magnetos — solid. He checked his carb heat — fine. Out of habit he set the altimeter at 675 feet for Yellowknife. He shook his head and a smile played at the corner of his lips.

"Now why the hell did I do that?"

His radio came to life.

"C-FCTQ you are cleared for takeoff."

"C-FCTQ. Roger. And thank you."

With one hand on the wheel, his other hand pushed the throttle full in and the aircraft leaped down the runway. The wheels accelerated far more quickly than floats or skis do, and in no time, Max was airborne for the first time in five years. The physical rush of it all was almost overwhelming and Max had to steady himself to prepare himself and his aircraft for the flight of a lifetime. He made a slow climbing bank to the left, leveled out at 3,000 feet and set his compass at 340 degrees, just west of North. That would put him close to, or over, Great Bear Lake later, depending on the fuel.

The ground fog had lifted as Dan and his family turned off the highway at that strange time when the night is neither dusk nor dark. The headlights found the parking place, and the dogs in the pens nearby voiced their usual welcome.

"I'm going to look in on the dogs. I'll see you at the cabin."

Akkisuktok was the first to see Ulysses sitting on the doorstep and she launched herself at him.

"Ulysses! ULYSSES! You're back! You're back. You're HERE!"

With Soleil only steps behind, the little girl threw her arms around the dog and buried her face in his fur and smelled the almost forgotten smell of his dogness. Her tears were absorbed by his magnificent white mane.

"Oh Ulysses," she sobbed. "Oh, Ulysses!"

Soleil fell to her knees and embraced both of them and contributed her joy to the welcome. Dan, who hadn't made it to the dog pens, stood silent and unbelieving. While mother, daughter and dog were reacquainting, the cabin door slowly opened. Soleil was startled and looked up. A sleepy-eyed Luna broke into a huge grin and threw herself at her sister. The sounds of screams of happiness and cries of unbridled joy filled the air. Akkis, confused by this unfamiliar woman, ran to her father and clutched his thigh. Dan cupped her cheek in his hand soothingly. The two women were lost in a frantic babble of half-questions and non-answers as they embraced and laughed and cried, creating a cacophony of joy and emotion.

"Dan, this is Luna who I told you about. Akkis, this is your aunt Luna. Say hello."

Akkis reluctantly let go of her father, and looking at the ground, took an unsteady step forward. She extended her tiny hand.

"How do you do, Aunt Luna. Pleased to meet you."

Luna exchanged a glance with Soleil then scooped the little girl up in her arms, spinning around and around. Akkis relaxed and began to giggle.

"We're family. We don't have to shake hands. We can hug and kiss all we want!"

Dan knelt before Ulysses and held his head in his strong hands. Man and beast looked into each other's eyes, and looked and looked.

"I don't know where they took you or how they kept you," Dan whispered, "but you're home now. If it took six months, it must have been a very long journey."

And for the first time in their history, Dan McCord hugged Ulysses. And Ulysses accepted it.

"Momma, Daddy, look!" And she pointed to the sky. Dan spoke first.

"The aurora. Unusual at this time of the year, but still beautiful."

He looked over at Soleil who was standing behind her sister, arms encircling her. They both gazed up in amazement. Luna stifled a tear.

"It is totally amazing. I haven't seen it for, well, it seems like forever. It's so great to be back."

"Why does it move like that, Daddy?"

"Well it starts with magnetic energy made by the sun that is thrown out into space. After traveling millions of miles, it reaches our earth and connects with small particles around it high in the sky, and the energy makes them glow."

"It's really beautiful, right Mommy?"

"It is darling, and some people believe the aurora has special spiritual qualities. People from Japan are convinced that children whose creation begins under the northern lights will be blessed and live long and successful lives. People on earth have been amazed and frightened by the aurora for a long, long time."

Soleil looked at everyone, and her gaze stopped at Ulysses. She was quiet for a moment.

"It has been a long day, especially for Luna and Ulysses, I expect. It's getting dark so let's go inside, put a log in the stove and start to catch up. I'll make something to eat. You must be hungry."

This was what Max had been missing. For the past five years he had not really been the master of his own destiny. But now he was. He was in complete control. That's how he felt at the controls of any aircraft. And he remembered the feeling of power and satisfaction that control used to give him. Domination even. He was dominating gravity. As he flew north, dusk began to fall, and the light changed quickly. The air in the cabin became cool so Max turned on the heater. The setting sun was behind him to his right and the cabin was washed with a warm yellow light that lasted only a few minutes. Though it was not yet pitch black, Max was flying into the night. He settled further into his seat and remembered what it meant to be at one with his airplane. It was peaceful. It was sweet. It was who he was. A movement in the night sky caught his attention. The Aurora Borealis. Massive curtains of flowing and undulating green light filled the windscreen of the little aircraft. Ever-changing, and ever more beautiful than the moment before, the shimmering sky transfixed Max with its mysterious beauty. Although he knew this band of electrically charged particles was a hundred miles above him, so large was the display that he felt he was flying into the very heart of it, that he was a part of it. That he was IT. He reached into the pocket of his coat and found the CD, which he slid into the deck in the control panel. A flashing red light on the instrument panel told him his fuel was low. He switched off the illumination. There was no information there he really needed to see. He pressed 'Play' and the opening bars of his beloved 'Lagrime di San Pietro' filled the cabin. Twenty-one voices in meticulous Medieval acapella polyphony touched Max's soul like no other sound he had ever known. He turned up the volume as far as it would go. If anything could raise him to tears, it was this. And combined with the incredible aurora dancing and shimmering in the sky, the experience was truly transcendental. In some part of his being Max felt the suffering of St. Peter for his disavowing Jesus Christ on the day of his arrest before his crucifixion. He, Max, had been disavowed by those sent to hurt him and kill him. He knew how it felt, he really did. And, like Jesus Christ, he didn't deserve it.

Max's reverie was interrupted by the engine coughing as it became starved of fuel. Then it stopped and the propeller froze at 11:00 o'clock. He barely paid attention to it other than to adjust the trim tabs to keep the airplane level as it sunk slowly and inexorably toward the earth silently obeying the immutable laws of lift and drag. With his music and

Nature's display both playing their melodies, Max had never felt more at peace with himself. It didn't matter when his flight ended, or where, or how. The outcome would be the same. Regrets? He had only two. That he had never been able to decode the mysteries of that magnificent white dog. The dog he hated for its perfection but came to love for its spirit. If things had been different and he had a little more time...

And the other was that he never learned the fate of the only person he ever loved, Lisa, and their child. They had met when he was a freshly minted pilot in Juneau. Their attraction was immediate and powerful. Six months later she discovered she was pregnant, and six months plus a day later, she vanished. He was devastated and spent the next two years searching for word of her. All he could learn was that she had returned to her Dene family near Yellowknife to give birth. A few years later there was a rumour that she had married, and a second child was expected. Max had wanted desperately to contact her but ultimately decided against it. After all, she had made her choice. And he still had his love of flying. He loved her birth name, always had. Liseli, a Chippewa name meaning 'light.' He caught his breath. His heart skipped a beat. Oh my God! Could it be that the mother Light created a Sun and a Moon? A Soleil and a Luna? Could it be possible that Lisa was...?! That would mean that Soleil is...

A white-tailed deer on the shoreline half a mile away saw a silhouette against the green aurora of a large, silent bird gradually approaching the water. Its feet touched the surface of the lake, then grabbed it, flipping it onto its back. There it hung for a few seconds, then quietly disappeared from view. The animal looked into the darkness for another heartbeat or two, then returned to foraging in the green grasses along the shoreline. The lake water licked at the rocks as it had been doing for a hundred years – and the rocks still hadn't changed.

The biggest event in Max Pfister's life had no more significance to it than the raindrop falling on the surface of the lake. And they both became one with the water.

Over dinner, Luna told them her story, starting with running away from the foster home, until now. While Soleil was washing the dishes, Ulysses became restless. He stood up, and walked in small circles, and sounded little muffled barks deep in his throat. He went to the door and jumped up on it. Akkis ran over.

"I'll let him out."

But instead of running into the forest as when urged by nature, he walked very slowly into the clearing in front of the cabin. The family stood in the doorway gazing at this unexpected and strange behaviour. Ulysses made two circles, as if orienting himself toward some unseen place. He raised his head to the shimmering green sky and howled a sorrowful, aching howl that sounded as if his heart was being pulled from his chest and thrown into the sky for all to see his pain. Soleil and Dan looked at one another. They had heard Ulysses make that sound before - when Dan's father died. Soleil nodded at Dan with her eyes. Luna's story had touched them both deeply, and it all began to make sense. They knew the who of it but not the where or the how. Soleil spoke as if reciting a prayer.

"Ulysses has lost someone who loved him very much."

Slowly, quietly, the family returned to the cabin. Ulysses refused to go in, preferring to curl up on the ground in front of the gently closed door. He laid down on exactly the same place where he lay on the first day he came to the cabin those five years ago. The night was quiet and still in stark contrast to all the recent sounds of happiness so freely shared with the forest and its inhabitants. A zephyr caressed the tips of the tops of the tallest trees. The aurora continued its swirling, sweeping dance in the sky as it had done for hundreds of thousands of years. The timeless energy of the cosmos still dictating the rhythms of nature and life on this tiny speck of dust in the galaxy called the Milky Way.

Perhaps it was these forces that had guided Ulysses on his seemingly impossible journey of well over two thousand miles through strange and unfamiliar places. Or perhaps it was love with its mystical connection that had pointed his way.

Ulysses eyes were heavy, and he fell asleep knowing he was home. And his heart and his soul were safe here in this place so filled with love.

EPILOGUE

AFTER THE FALL OF TROY, ODYSSEUS (KNOWN TO THE ROMANS AS *Ulysses*) *set sail back to Ithaca and his beloved wife Penelope. In his wildest imagination he could never have known that his odyssey would take him 10 years. On his way he would encounter many strange sights and dangerous situations. Among them, the giant one-eyed Cyclops and the rock-throwing Laestragonians. He would be seduced by the alluring songs of the Sirens and their sensual way of life. Determined to be reunited with his wife, he pulled himself away only to be confronted with the choice of navigating through giant rocks, or swimming across a wide and deep river where he would encounter a deadly whirlpool. Finally arriving home, he was unable to recognize his island as it was shrouded in mist. But finally, as all good stores must end, Ulysses was reunited with his beloved and beautiful wife Penelope, whose love was strong, and who had waited for him for so many years.*

A SONG

"FOLLOWING THE LOVE"

The sound of Inuit throat singers and First Nations drumming can be heard in the background.

    A thousand miles before me lie strange and dangerous lands,
    The days are long and dry and hot, the sunshine bakes the sand.

    Moonshine is my faithful beacon and she becomes my guide
    To the family I am seeking, seeking, and the love I feel inside.

    The mountains call and promise peace and rivers cool and swift,
    My journey must go on and on for love is the Spirit Guide's gift.

    Following the love,
    Following my heart,
    I'm following the love
    To home.

    Comin' Home.
    Comin' Home.
    I'm comin' Ho… Ho… Ho… *(wolf howl)*… Home.

"FOLLOWING THE LOVE"

The wet and shiny highway stretches miles to who knows where.
Beyond the endless horizon the ones I love are there.

The days are long and lonely, the nights are dark and cold,
The road goes on forever and my soul is feeling old.

But the call of love keeps driving me to the home where I need to be.
My heart is weary, my body aches, crying out for my family.

Following the love,
Following my heart,
I'm following the love
To home.

Comin' Home.
Comin' Home.
I'm comin' Ho... Ho... Ho... *(wolf howl)*... Home.

© 2021 Maybe Tomorrow Music

CPSIA information can be obtained
at www.ICGtesting.com
Printed in the USA
LVHW111920060621
689455LV00016B/813